SKATEBOARD

Novelization
by
Gail Kimberly

A Tempo Star Book

Distributed by Ace Books

GROSSET & DUNLAP
A FILMWAYS COMPANY
Publishers ● New York

ISBN: 0-441-76875-3

A Tempo Books Original
Tempo Books is registered in the U.S. Patent Office

Printed in the United States of America

Acknowledgments

My special thanks to Glenn and Eve Bunting, authors of *Skateboards, How to Make Them, How to Ride Them* (Harvey House, New York), and to Nathan "Chip" Wolfstein IV, author of *Skateboard Safety* (Skateboard Safety Publications, Sherman Oaks, California) for their advice and information; to Skateboard World Park, Torrance, California, for their hospitality and assistance; to the skateboarders who told me such a lot about skateboarding and demonstrated their skills; to Gloria Miklowitz, Shirley Skelton, and Evelyn and Kip Kimberly, who helped so much during the writing of this book, and to Suzanne R. Blum for an added measure of assistance.

Introduction

Maybe you've heard of the Los Angeles Wheels, the skateboard team? That's us . . . seven of us plus our manager, Manny Bloom, and our team nurse, Millicent Broderick.

You might know our names, if you're into skateboarding, or even our specialties: Jenny Bradshaw and Randi Peterson, the girls on the team who are champs at freestyle skating; Tony Bluetile, a kid who'll ride just about anything on a dare, he's broken the world record for jumping barrels, eighteen of them; Peter Steffens, always chewing on a wad of bubble gum, who's famous for daredevil stunts like jumping cars; Dennis Wagstaff, ten years old, who can skate rings around guys a lot older; Jason Maddox, who's a champion surfer as well as our star skateboarder; and me, Brad Harris, the one who has the most to learn. I catch on pretty fast though and so far downhill is what I like best.

There's a song called "Skate Out" that has a particular meaning for us.

We are children of the new beginning
Changing with the tides of time
Breaking through the walls of darkness

Soaring high into the skies
Skate out—skate out

Flying high and you can't touch us
We're moving too fast for you
Gotta know that you can't stop us
Step aside we're comin' on through
Skate out—skate out

Here we are, all together
Unafraid we're on our way
Searching for our own tomorrows
Ridin' on the winds of change
*Skate out—skate out**

That song does a good job of describing how we feel, as skateboarders and as a team. We're all together, but we're searching for our own tomorrows.

Maybe you know all about our team. We've performed in a lot of places. But maybe you don't know our real, inside story. Nothing came easy for us, especially for Manny, who had to face some dangerous opposition getting the team formed and started on its way up. In fact, the opposition was out to kill him.

He wasn't the only one who had problems. Jason had a bad time that almost spelled the end of the L.A. Wheels, and I had a few troubles of my own. But even I didn't know the whole story until it was all over.

It all began one day last June. . . .

Chapter 1

The phone next to Manny Bloom's bed rang three seconds before his clock radio burst into music.

Manny swung his well-padded body out of the bed, yawned, scratched his head, and glanced at the digits on the clock—8:00A.M. *If they're going to start phoning at this hour, I might as well hock the clock radio,* he thought as he walked into the living room. *I could use the money.* Ignoring the litter of old newspapers, back issues of *Daily Variety* and *The Hollywood Reporter* that covered every available horizontal surface, Manny spotted a half-eaten donut on a table and ate it absently as he headed for the kitchen. He also ignored the phone. Anyone calling before he had his morning shot of Mountain Dew deserved to be ignored.

Whoever was calling was persistent. The phone nagged at him several more times while he shaved and dressed, and he could hear it ringing again as he went out the apartment door. It didn't stop him. Clients should know his business day didn't start until nine, and if it wasn't a client, it wasn't anyone he wanted to talk to.

As he got into his car, Manny noted the cloudless, smogless blue skies and the refreshing breeze. Maybe this beautiful day was a good omen. Maybe today would be the day he could figure a way out of the mess he was in. But then, the last time he'd thought he had a good omen was in the fourth race at Hollywood Park ... a horse named Lucky Emanuel ... who'd ended up running the race like it was a stroll through the park.

Manny walked to his '67 Datsun convertible which was parked facing up a steep hill. He banged his leg as he got in and muttered a prayer that the car would start. It did—barely. He started up and at the intersection he slowed as he approached a stop sign, when suddenly something zoomed out of the side road and came at him full tilt. Manny's foot jammed on the brake and the tires screeched, but the kid on the skateboard streaking straight for him didn't stop. Manny held his breath and clutched the steering wheel. He watched, horrified, and saw the kid crouch and leap right over the hood of his car, then land easily on the skateboard that had rolled under it and come out on the other side at the same time the kid landed. After this hair-raising maneuver, the kid straightened and halted his skateboard, then turned to grin at Manny.

It took a minute before Manny's hands relaxed enough to come loose from the steering wheel and he could stick his head out the window. Then he let all his indignation out in one huge bellow.

"Hey! What do you think you're doing?"

The kid gave no sign that he had heard. He

stepped casually back on the skateboard and rolled away.

Manny tried to get out of the car but his seat belt held him tightly. As he struggled with it, a boy and girl, both on skateboards, rolled up beside his car and quickly cut in front of it before they zoomed away around the corner.

Irritated, Manny looked helplessly after them until a loud honking jarred him to the realization that he was holding up traffic at the stop sign, and if he didn't hurry he'd be late for his appointment at the unemployment office.

There were long lines of people waiting. There seemed to be crowds at the Hollywood unemployment office no matter how early or late he came. Manny glanced through the glass door, then went to the newspaper dispenser and bought a *Los Angeles Times*. He opened the door, took his place at the end of the middle line, and fumbled through the paper for the sports section.

The man in front of him, a tall dude wearing a broad-brimmed hat and cowboy boots, turned, "Hey, Manny! Anything going down?"

Manny looked up from his paper into the dilated pupils and vaguely smiling face of Vito Visconsi, the friendly local pusher.

"Nothing good," he said, running his finger down a column in the paper. "My nag lost to a 30-to-1 shot." First those skateboarders, and now this. And he'd thought the day was a good omen! He sighed. "Can't pick a winner, and I can't sell a client these days."

Vito looked at him beatifically. "Console yourself, Manny. I got some very bad weed, man. I got some Mowie Wowie—"

"Mowie? Frankly, Vito, I've got a lot of pressures on my mind right now."

"Then how about some raw San Sinsemillan? Get you high."

Manny shook his head. "With what I'm paying my old lady for alimony, I can hardly afford a can of Mountain Dew."

"Listen, man," Vito said. "You smoke some of this herb and you won't care about alimony."

"I'm not interested in that garbage, Vito," Manny said firmly. "That was my old lady, remember?"

"Next!" the clerk at the glass window called.

Vito turned around and stepped forward while Manny folded the sports section and put it in the pocket of his jacket, noting as he did so that the seams of the pocket were ripped.

The clerk dealing with Vito was writing something on a pad in front of him. Vito talked over his shoulder to Manny. "Listen, when I run into your old lady, I'll tell her you said hi, okay?"

"Sure."

"In two weeks," the clerk told Vito.

Vito turned and walked past Manny. "Stay high, Manny!"

"Take care of yourself, Vito." Manny stepped up to the window. He dropped the rest of his newspaper in the trash basket next to him and tried to look earnest.

"Ah, Mr. Blum," the clerk said.

"Yeah, right."

"Please sign on the 'X'."

"In two weeks," the man, who had a very large

nose and fascinating face, repeated.

"Say, ah . . . what . . . you forgot my check," Manny insisted.

"Sorry."

"Thank you," Manny turned to walk away.

"Two weeks."

"Yeah," Manny continued. "Listen, ah . . . do you ever do any acting?"

"Me? Acting? Oh, I don't think I have the face for it."

"Yeah," Manny said, chuckling to himself. "You're probably right."

The mailman had already been there when he got back to his apartment house. There were a couple of overdue bills, an ad, and a manila envelope addressed in a feminine hand to the Emanuel Bloom Agency for the Performing Arts. Manny stood in front of his door and ripped open the envelope. Maybe this one would be the one he was always hoping for—someone with looks and talent —someone he could guide into movies or TV who would make money for him along the way. But the picture he pulled out was the usual. An overweight, fortyish blonde in a bikini. And there was the usual note enclosed that read: "I've always wanted to be an actress, Mr. Bloom, but never had the opportunity . . ." Manny snorted, put his key in the lock, and went inside. He was an agent, not a miracle worker, and considering the number of salable clients he had at the moment, he wasn't even an agent. Zero, that was the number.

The phone was ringing again as he entered the

apartment, or maybe it was still ringing. Manny tossed the mail on his desk and picked up the receiver.

"Good morning. E.B.A.," he said in a high voice he hoped sounded like a female secretary. Appearances were everything in this business.

"Manny, is that you?" His ex-wife's voice was irritable, as always.

"Do you want Mr. Bloom?" Manny kept on in the female voice. "I'll check to see if he's in." The falsetto cracked a little, and Manny squirmed. He put down the phone, took a deep breath to calm himself, then picked it up again. "I'm sorry, Mrs. Bloom. I think he's left for the day."

"Manny, I know it's you."

He dropped the receiver on its hook and sat at his desk, frowning. She wanted to nag him about the alimony he owed her, that was for sure. Well, he'd send it to her if he could ever get his hands on some. Right now he didn't even have enough for a decent breakfast until he cashed his unemployment check, and all *that* money had to go on his overdue bills. He searched through the papers on his desk, found a jar of peanuts, and took a handful.

The phone rang again and he picked it up. Maybe this one would be good news. "Good morning. E.B.A.," he said in the same female voice.

"Don't try that phony secretary routine on me, Manny," said the deep voice on the other end of the line, and Manny could feel cold sweat breaking out on his forehead. He tried to sound pleased.

"Hey, Sol, whaddya say, buddy?"

Sol's voice was dry and cold. "You owe me, baby. That's what I say."

"Sol . . . Sol! How long have we known each other?"

"Longer than my accountant says we should have."

"Oh, Sol, just give me a little more time. That's all I need. Just a little more time. I'm on to something really big, Solly."

"What is it?"

Manny tried to think up something, fast, but nothing occurred to him. He was too uptight. He tried evasion. "I don't know if it's such a good idea to talk about this on the phone. And it's going to take some cash, Sol—"

"Hey, hey!" Sol interrupted. "Don't try to con me, Buddha Belly. What is this big idea?"

He had to come up with something, quick. You didn't mess around with Sol. Manny picked through his mind for an idea . . . something, *anything* that would pacify Sol. . . . But the only thing in his head was the memory of those kids on skateboards he'd seen earlier this morning . . . the guy who had jumped over the hood of his car, and the other two.

Wait a minute! Kids on skateboards! There was his answer.

"The youth market, Sol!"

"The youth market?" Sol sounded anything but enthusiastic. "What are you talking about? How am I supposed to make money on the youth market?"

"It's hot," Manny told him eagerly. "There are disco contests, frisbee olympics . . . even hula hoops are coming back. What's the matter, don't you read the papers?"

"Yeah, I read. I read plenty. I don't read much about the youth market, but I read how you're not balancing on my books." Sol's voice rose to an angry shout. "You owe me sixty-five hundred dollars, Manny! So tell me how I'm going to make it back on the youth market."

Manny paced back and forth, holding the phone in a sweating hand, feeling like a drowning man going down for the third time. The word came out of him like a cry of despair. "Skateboards!"

The silence on the other end of the line was long and uncomfortable. Finally Sol's voice, faint and skeptical now, came through. "Skateboards! Those things the kids ride!"

"Right. They've really taken off, Sol. They're the biggest thing on wheels."

Another long silence. "How much is *this* going to cost me?"

Manny began to relax a little. Sol was going for it! "About two ... uh ... three thousand, Sol. That would get it off the ground. And then I'll pay you the whole ninety-five hundred plus interest in a couple of months. How's that!"

Sol sounded doubtful. "That would mean you'd owe me ten thousand, Manny."

But he hadn't refused. Manny knew he was considering it now. He made his voice sound as sincere and enthusiastic as a TV pitchman's. "There's real money in this, Solly. We're talking about a lot more than ten thousand. If you'll meet me at the usual place tomorrow night, I can tell you all the details."

"Okay," Sol said, "but just remember this. You try to con me and you're going to come down with a bad case of poor health." The click at Sol's end of the line sounded like a gunshot.

Manny put down the phone with shaking hands. At least he'd convinced Sol to give him more time and more money. But Sol knew Manny didn't have anywhere near the money to pay for all his gambling debts—not sixty-five hundred dollars' worth. Sol knew that to get the money back he'd have to trust Manny a little way, invest some money, and make it back with a profit big enough to erase the debt, with maybe a little left over. Manny knew exactly how Sol's mind was working, and he also knew Sol meant what he said. He might go along with Manny this far, but there was no way Manny could get out of paying off Sol in the long run. Sol would see him dead first.

So now all Manny had to do was get all the details of his scheme ready to present to Sol. To get those details, all he had to do was find three kids he'd seen once on skateboards on a Hollywood street.

Chapter 2

It was a nightmare that woke me next morning. I was dreaming of riding my skateboard down the Matterhorn at Disneyland, trying to escape from a couple of monsters crammed into one of the little cars, chasing right on my tail. I could hear them shrieking, and I could even feel their breath on the back of my neck, and just when I knew they were going to grab me, I woke up. Must have been that Creature Feature I watched the night before.

I lay for a while, feeling my heart pounding. There was a warm patch of sunlight falling on my arms, and I could hear a purring sound coming from our driveway in front of the house. Skateboard wheels! Jenny and Tony were out there already.

I jumped out of bed and pulled on my jeans and a sweatshirt, and then I looked for the new sneakers I'd bought a couple of days ago. They were still in their box. I'd shoved them on the bottom shelf of my bookcase, under my stereo. I put them on and went downstairs, heading for the

front door, itching to be out there in the morning
sunshine riding my board. But Mom was too fast
for me. She was standing in the kitchen doorway,
watching me.

"Aren't you going to eat your breakfast, Brad?"

"I'm not hungry," I told her.

"Scrambled eggs and bacon? Already made.
Won't take you a minute to eat them."

I turned and went back down the hall, and sat
down at the kitchen table in front of a heaped-up
plate of bacon and eggs. I gulped down some orange juice and jabbed my fork around in the eggs.

"I've got to go, Mom. Tony and Jenny are out
there waiting."

She didn't understand. She seemed to think
there was something wrong with her cooking. She
stood beside the stove looking worried, her gray
hair curling around her face, wiping one very clean
hand on her apron. I didn't like to see her looking
worried like that, but she and my dad never seemed
to understand. They'd forgotten, if they ever knew,
what it was like when you were a teen-ager and the
morning was fresh and new, and there was a
skateboard gliding smoothly under your feet. I
don't think they even had skateboards when Mom
and Dad were teen-agers, at least not as good as
the ones now.

"These eggs are good," I told her, and she
smiled. I crammed a forkful into my mouth.

"You going skateboarding today?" she asked
me.

"Yeah."

"You're not going to take any foolish risks, are
you, Brad?"

"Of course not, Mom." Both of them were worried that I might get hurt. They'd heard about some skateboarders being bruised and scraped pretty badly—some had even broken bones—but I explained to them that usually happened only when you weren't dressed properly, or you took dumb chances when you weren't ready for them. I wear jeans and long-sleeved shirts when I'm just practicing freestyle tricks, but I always wear knee and elbow pads, gloves, and a helmet if I'm going to be skating fast. It doesn't make sense if you don't protect your body and your head. Also, I've got grip tape on my boards, and I tune them up regularly to make sure everything works the way it should. My folks know I'm careful; they just worry a lot about me. I'm their only child, and they were both pretty old when they had me, so they tend to be overprotective, I guess. They also expect me to be good at everything—you know. It seems as if all their hopes and dreams center on me because I'm all they have. That's pretty heavy to live up to believe me. Sometimes I feel like I don't want them butting into everything I do. I want to be free and I want to be me.

I grabbed a slice of crisp bacon for the road, and split.

Tony and Jenny were just outside, practicing wheelies on the road in front of the house. We have a big old house with a long, curving driveway that slopes down toward the street, and the neighborhood is quiet so you don't have to worry much about traffic. Where Tony lives, in an apartment near Hollywood Boulevard, you'd be killed if you took your board off the sidewalk.

Jenny is real good at wheelies. She was doing nose wheelies, the skateboard standing still, its rear wheels in the air, while she balanced like a tightrope walker on the front of it. She told me once she'd studied ballet and was on the gymnastics team at school. She felt that helped to give her good balance.

Tony was doing tail wheelies. You can do wheelies with either both feet on the board or only one. He was doing a one-foot wheelie, his right foot centered over the rear wheels of the board, his left leg bent, and his arms out for balance.

I grabbed up my board beside the front door and skated down the driveway toward them. When Jenny saw me she smiled and waved, but Tony just kept doing wheelies, staring at nothing. It's not that he isn't friendly; he's just a loner. He only goes along with the other guys when he feels like it, and most of the time he likes to be by himself. But he's out of sight on a skateboard, and so is Jenny. I felt good that I could keep up with them . . . that they let me skate with them. I got my first skateboard four years ago, and took to it right away. I'm nowhere near as good as Tony or Jason, but I can hold my own, especially on this new board my dad just got me. It's custom-made birch with "Stokersize" wheels, and it rides like a surfboard on a soft wave. As long as they let me hang out with them I figured I'd at least learn some new stuff.

For a while I practiced wheelies with them until Tony started talking about heading over to the pool. We were tossing the idea around when this crummy-looking old silver sports car passed us. The driver stuck his head out the window and stared at us, then pulled suddenly into our driveway and jumped out of the car. He was fat and dark-haired, and he looked excited.

"Hey!" he called as he came toward us. "You're the kids I saw yesterday. You remember me?"

"Not really," Tony said.

I didn't recognize him either, but we'd been out on our boards yesterday. Maybe he had seen us. I wondered if he had some beef about us skateboarding past his house making too much noise or something.

He looked around. "There was a kid with you yesterday who jumped over my car."

He had to mean Peter, and I remembered then. Peter had jumped this guy's car at a stop sign.

"I think he's riding pools," Tony told him cautiously.

The guy seemed really happy about finding us. "Can he do that all the time . . . jump over cars? I mean, what's the percentage?"

"Percentage?" Jenny looked puzzled. "He can do it any time he wants to."

He seemed impressed. "Really? What about you kids, can you do stuff like that?"

"We're all into different things," Tony said.

"Yeah." Jenny did another nose wheelie for him. "Freestyle, you know. Like handstands, nose wheelies, three-sixties."

He didn't seem to get what she was talking about; he just said "Yeah?" and then nodded thoughtfully. "I'm Emanuel Bloom." He held out his hand to me. "Call me Manny."

"I'm Brad Harris." I shook his hand, which was warm and sweaty. "This is Jenny Bradshaw and Tony Bluetile."

He shook hands with the others while we all

wondered what his angle was. He seemed to be leading up to something, but we couldn't guess what.

Then he told us. "What if I were to organize a team?"

Jenny looked at me, and I knew what she was thinking. This guy thought he'd just had the greatest idea in the world.

"You'd be just another guy with a skateboard team," I told him.

He looked surprised. "There are other teams?"

"Sure," I said. "Lots of them."

"My team's going to be different."

Tony looked at him suspiciously. "Yeah? How?"

"I'm going to pay you. You'll be pros."

Tony grinned and Jenny raised her eyebrows. We all just about laughed out loud. This guy was driving an old, beat-up sports car with a dented rear fender. He was wearing a jacket that looked like something my dad would give to the Salvation Army, and his pants and those scuffed, run-down loafers he was wearing weren't too neat either.

I couldn't help saying it. "Doesn't look like you'll be paying us much."

He noticed how we were looking at him. "Please. Don't go by the car or these clothes. I like to keep a low profile."

"Real low." Tony agreed.

Manny was scratching his curly hair and his eyes were taking all of us in like we were three juicy pork chops. "I've got to find some more kids as good as you."

Jenny tossed her blonde curls. She isn't really

conceited, but she was putting this guy on. "That could be hard," she said.

He took her seriously. "I'm sure I can handle it."

He did seem to mean what he said about organizing a pro team. I thought we should at least find out what was on his brain.

"We know a couple of others," I said.

"Who's that?"

"A couple of pretty hot skateboarders we know. We could take you to see them if you want." I knew Jason would probably be over at the empty pool about this time of day. He knew about this neat empty pool in the neighborhood that we could sneak into to practice some hot bank riding. The people who lived there both worked and we never got caught. I looked at Tony and Jenny to see if they wanted to do it. "Think we should take him to the pool?"

Tony must have decided the same thing I did, that we should give Manny a chance to explain his big scheme. He picked up his skateboard. "Sure," he said. "We can take you there, man. Let's go."

"Do we get a ride over there with you?" Jenny asked.

Manny opened his car door for us. "You get a ride, but you'll have to sit on the floor. I've only got one seat."

"Unreal!" Jenny and I sat on the floor while Tony got up on the top of the deck lid, after he pulled down the portable convertible top.

"It's the only car I've got," Manny said. "Don't break it!" He backed it out of the driveway. "These guys we're going to see are pretty good, are they?"

"Wait till you see Jason," Tony said, gripping the edge of the folded-down top for support. "He'll blow you away!"

"What's so good about him?"

"He's just about the hottest downhill racer in California, that's all."

That was true. Everybody knew it. But what we didn't tell Manny was that Jason went his own way. I don't think any of us really understood him.

Manny would have to find that out for himself.

Chapter 3

Jason Maddox woke to the smell of frying Spam.

He sat up, glanced over at Scott's bed and saw that it was empty, then pulled back the red curtain that blanked out the window beside his own bed. The ocean was smooth this morning. Not much surf, just gently lapping waves that left frothy lace tracks on the sand. He dropped the curtain, got out of bed, and went through the tiny living room into the even tinier kitchen. His brother Scott was standing there, toasting bread on a fork over a gas flame.

"Any of that left for me?" Jason asked.

"Sure. There's some eggs, too. I bought them yesterday." Scott set his paper plate on the miniature table and sat down in the only chair.

Jason sliced some Spam and put it in the frying pan. "You leaving for work already?"

"Yeah, I have to start at eight today. The store manager changed all the hours around yesterday. Now he wants me to get the produce ready first thing in the morning."

"Did he say anything about hiring me?"

"Not yet. When did you get your application in?"

"Last week. Thursday, I think." Jason broke an egg over the Spam slices and watched the clear part of it turn white. He had to get a job. He needed the bread to buy a car for himself, and to take Randi out someplace nice for a change. Scott had been good about paying the rent and the utility bills himself and buying the groceries, but that was because Scott had always felt responsible for Jason, ever since their mother had died eight years ago when Jason was ten, and their father hadn't had the time or the money to give either one of his boys much more than the bare necessities. Now Scott was twenty, and he'd had this pad on the beach for three years. He'd quit school to go to work and pay for it. Now that Jason had graduated from high school, he wanted to pay his share. He wasn't going to think about college. Not yet. But maybe later, when he got a job and had something saved. Maybe he could try for a scholarship then, too. He'd work it out. For sure his dad couldn't help him. He'd been happy enough to see them grow up and go out on their own. No, Jason could work it out himself.

Scott finished his breakfast and went into the bedroom to dress.

"Can I have the van today?" Jason called to him through a mouthful of Spam and egg.

"Okay, but you'll have to drive me to work." Scott came out of the bedroom, pulling on his shirt. "And pick me up at *five,* not five after."

"Right." Jason finished the Spam and followed his brother outside, around the little house to the alley behind it where the van was kept. It was painted a glorious bronze-brown, like a deep suntan, and Scott had had it pinstriped so that it looked like no other van on the beach. Scott would never lend it to anyone except Jason.

"Check that left rear tire," Scott warned him as he got out at the supermarket where he worked.

Jason nodded. "See you later."

He headed the van for Hollywood, for a vacant house he knew of there. It had an empty swimming pool that was great for skateboarding.

Peter Steffens was already there, and Jason got his skateboard from the back of the van and went down the pool steps. Then he glided from the shallow end to the deep end and around the pool, picking up speed. He was really going great when the others arrived, riding the banked sides of the pool, and turned on so much by the excitement and danger of climbing the almost-vertical walls that he barely noticed them standing on the edge, watching him. When he finally saw the stranger standing with Brad, Jenny, and Tony, looking at him as though he'd been hypnotized, Jason treated him to a long, crouching run to the deep end and then a climb up the wall to the blue tiles, until the watchers were whooping and the stranger was popeyed.

Man, this was it! Jason knew he was good . . . the hottest thing on wheels if you wanted the truth . . . and he had never had this same feeling doing anything else, even surfing. Sure it was neat to catch a big wave and ride it in to shore, but you still had to let the wave carry you. You were at its mercy. Skateboarding like this, he was in complete control, doing it all himself, his body coordinating perfectly with the rhythm—the feel—of the skateboard and the surface under it. Riding the board, his mind could really get onto a natural high, and he could let it soar into exhilaration he had never felt any other way. Freedom ... intoxication ... tripping out ...

He saw the stranger with Brad shaking his head in disbelief, and he could hear them talking, their words resounding through the bowl of the empty pool, over the hum of his and Peter's wheels.

"What am I supposed to do?" the stranger said. "Build a swimming pool for every show?"

"No sweat. Jason can skate anywhere." That was Brad's voice.

"Will he do it?"

Jason couldn't hear the answer to that.

"Why wouldn't he? Couldn't he use the bread?"

"He could definitely use the bread." Brad's voice again. "It's just that sometimes Jason's weird, you know?"

"What do you mean? Drugs?" the stranger was asking.

"Are you kidding. No way, man! Just the opposite. Jason's really into his own head. When he's riding, he's out there ... you know?"

Jason flipped out of the pool to see what was going on. Tony ran down the steps, carrying his skateboard, and raced across the blue cement bottom of the pool, criss-crossing Peter's tracks so that the two of them performed an intricate dance.

"What's shaking?" Jason asked Brad.

"This is Manny Bloom," Brad told him, and the stranger held out a hand to shake Jason's.

"I'd like to talk to you about joining the Los Angeles Wheels," Manny said. His manner reminded Jason of a used-car salesman.

"Who are they?"

"My new skateboard team."

Jason pushed his skateboard back and forth with one foot. "You do this for a living?"

"Well . . . not exactly," Manny said. "I'm an agent, but my business isn't so great these days. I'm going to promote something new. How about it?"

Jason picked up his board, disappointed. For a minute he'd thought there might be something good going down. "No way, José," he said and turned toward the van. Best he split this scene.

But Brad called after him excitedly. "Hey, wait a minute Jason! This is a *professional* skateboard team!"

Jason stopped and turned back. "Pro? I've never heard of them."

"That's because they're just being formed." Manny waved a hand to indicate Brad, Jenny, Tony, and Peter. "These guys say you're the best skateboarder around."

Jason felt his interest growing. "Yeah? Well, they're pretty hot themselves."

"How do you like the idea?" Manny asked him.

"I don't know." Jason looked Manny over, noting that he didn't exactly look as if he were rolling in money. "How much do professional skateboarders make?"

"It depends."

"On what?"

"On what kind of a deal we work out," Manny said.

"First of all," Jason said, "who's on this team?"

"Brad and Tony and Jenny . . ." Manny pointed to each of them.

"I know Peter'll be stoked on it," Brad said. "And that little kid, Dennis . . ."

Jason thought it over. This might end up as a big joke, or it might pay off. This Manny guy seemed pretty confident. And getting paid for skateboarding would sure beat working in a grocery store.

"Okay," he said finally. "If you want me on your team, part of the deal is you hire my old lady, too."

Manny looked pained. "Listen, I'm not running a charity ward."

"Don't sweat it, man. My old lady doesn't need charity."

Brad grinned and nodded. "For sure!"

Manny looked at him doubtfully. "I'll have to meet her first."

"Sure," Jason said. "Follow me. I'm going to go meet her right now."

"Let's stop and pick up Dennis on the way," Brad said.

He and Jenny got into Manny's car, and Peter and Tony piled in beside Jason. All the way to Zuma Beach, Jason talked with them about Manny and his idea, getting more enthusiastic as they thought of the places they could travel and the money they could make. He nosed the van into a parking spot close to the beach and waited until Manny brought his old sports car up beside him. Then they all walked across the sand.

Randi was out there, all right. Jason recognized her bright yellow bikini and her tanned, slender compact body. She was crouching on her surfboard waiting for a wave, and just as Jason shouted and beckoned her to come in, the wave rose. Randi stood up on her surfboard and rode it in, her long legs steady and certain, her agile, athletic frame graceful and limber.

"Well," Manny said beside him, "at least she can surf."

"Wait until you see her. She's even better on concrete."

Randi came out of the water, carrying her surfboard, and Jason ran to meet her. He took the surfboard from her, placed it on the sand, and then he kissed her. She was cool and wet, and her mouth tasted salty. Jason led her towards Manny. "This is Manny Bloom."

Randi smiled.

"Just call me Manny."

"Manny's an agent," Jason told her.

Randi looked him over coolly. "Secret, government, or FBI?"

"Talent," Manny grinned. "I've got a business proposition for you."

Randi looked up at Jason, mystified.

"It's okay," he told her. "It's legit. In fact, I think it's a radical idea." He could see goose pimples breaking out on her skin, and he put his arm around her. "Come on, grab your stuff. We're all going to Neptune's Net. We can talk there."

"What kind of food do they serve?" Manny asked.

"Oysters."

"Good. I always talk better when I eat," Manny said.

Jason smiled and some of the other kids laughed. From the size of Manny's stomach, they all thought he must do a lot of good talking.

Chapter 4

Neptune's Net turned out to be an outdoor restaurant right on the beach. The thought of the fresh oysters they served here was making Manny's mouth water. He joined the kids, who were standing waiting as a well-built man in a T-shirt and apron scooped oysters from a cement tub onto an old scale, took a few away, and then dumped the remainder onto a paper plate.

Jason had gone to get the drinks, and now the man behind the counter was waiting to be paid, and the kids were all looking expectantly at Manny. He sighed, reached into his pocket, and slowly pulled out a few bills and some change. It was all he had with him, and he put it on the counter.

The T-shirted man counted it and shook his head. "Need a dollar more."

Manny looked at the group around him. "Can anyone lend me a dollar? I'm a little short."

"I don't believe it," Jason said, behind him. Manny turned to see that he'd brought some drinks and was putting them down on one of the redwood tables. "Do you think this guy's for real?" whispered Randi in his ear. Jason hesitated a minute. "Yea, I get pretty good vibes from him." He pulled some money from his pocket and tossed it to Manny.

"Thanks," Manny said. "Pay you back tomorrow."

They all sat at the redwood table under a naked light bulb, the younger kids grabbing cans of soft drinks, Jason and Randi with a tall, frosty pitcher in front of them. They had all taken paper plates from a stack on the counter, and now they helped themselves to oysters, Manny heaping his plate high.

"Don't they have Mountain Dew?" he asked Jason.

"Nope. How about some beer?"

"Just a smidgin," Manny said, holding out a paper cup.

Jason poured it half full.

Manny shoveled oysters into his mouth. "We'll get some uniforms . . . something flashy, you know?"

"How about blue ones?" Jenny asked. "I like blue."

"No," Manny said thoughtfully, watching the mosquitoes overhead make kamikaze runs on the light bulb. "Flashier than just blue."

Dennis, whom they'd picked up on the way here, and who seemed all excited about the idea, put a foot up on the bench. "What about like this?" His green-and-yellow sneaker glowed in the dim light.

"That's it!" Manny gulped down another oyster excitedly. "Those exact colors! And we'll have to get knee pads . . . right, Jason?"

Jason nodded. "Knee and elbow pads, and gloves."

Manny scooped up an especially large oyster. "Those will all be the same color, and T-shirts the same color as the shoes, with our name in some funky lettering. The Los Angeles Wheels." He belched happily. "We'll fill arenas . . . travel up and down the coast."

"San Francisco?" Jenny asked, her eyes shining.

"Big Sur and San Diego and Sacramento," Brad said.

"We've got to have helmets, too," Jason said.

"Helmets?" Manny suddenly remembered he was going to have to pay for all this. "How much do they cost?"

"Fifteen, twenty bucks," Tony told him.

"That much?"

"Hey, I thought you were big time, man!" Tony said.

"Hey, you don't know Manny Bloom," Manny said. "Nothing's too good for this team." He devoured another oyster to comfort himself. This was going to cost plenty. Maybe he should ask Sol for more money. But no . . . Sol wouldn't like that. He'd already said three thousand, and he wouldn't go for more, Manny was sure. He'd just have to cut down on expenses somehow.

Dennis had finished eating and was skateboarding among the tables.

"Come over here, Dennis. We're still talking business." Manny gulped down another oyster. "They'll probably want us for a tour back east, too. They're into skateboarding back there, aren't they?"

"I think so," Jenny said.

"Anybody tuned in is," Brad said.

"Yeah, man!" Tony waved his hands to encompass the whole world. "It's hot everywhere."

"Look," Manny said, "I know it is. There's no end to it. We could appear on the Sports Spectacular, the Wide World of Sports, all those things. There'd be enough for them to cover, wouldn't there?"

"Sure, there's all kinds of things," Peter said.

"Yeah? Like what?"

"Like freestyle," Jenny said. "And slalom races."

Manny looked around at the group. "Can *all* of you do all of that?"

"We can all do them," Brad told him, "but some of us are more into things, you know?"

Tony nodded. "Yeah, like barrel jumping."

"Or pool riding," Jason said.

Peter agreed. "Pool riding's where it's at."

"Listen," Manny told them sternly, "you guys may like pools, but I've got to put on a show, too."

"That's cool," Brad told him. "We could put on a show at one of the skate parks."

Jason nodded. "Some of the bowls at Montebello are pretty radical."

Manny nervously speared an oyster on his fork. "Can't you do anything without a swimming pool or a skate park?"

Tony hooted. "Listen, man, if it's smooth, I'll skate anywhere."

"Yeah, but how are we going to get to all those places?" Brad asked. "None of us have wheels."

"You have a van, don't you?" Manny asked Jason.

"No way, man. That's my brother's, and he'll kill me if he finds out I've taken all of you guys out in it."

Manny swallowed the oyster, thinking hard. He was pretty sure he knew where he would get something to travel in. He'd have to work on it. Getting the team together was the most important part, and here they all were . . . all willing and able. The uniforms, helmets, and transportation could be worked out. "Come on," he said. "I'd better get you kids out of here. I'll be in trouble with your parents before this team ever gets started."

"And I've got to get over and pick up my brother," Jason said.

"Okay," Manny said. "We'll meet day after tomorrow somewhere and I'll have some more to tell you. In the meantime, talk to your folks about our plans. Then tell them I'd like to meet with them and get their permission. Where's a good meeting place?"

"You can come to my house," Brad offered.

"Okay, we meet at noon in Brad's house."

As Jason and Randi headed for the van and the other kids went to get into his Datsun, Manny picked up the paper plate with the remaining oysters. There was his dinner. He was going to see Sol later for money, but he'd need it all to finance his team. The thought made him feel good. *His team!* Seven talented kids. He was betting on seven kids on skateboards to save his neck with Sol. He was staking his life on them.

But then, he was a gambler, wasn't he?

Chapter 5

Jason felt uncomfortable sitting in Brad's living room beside Randi, watching all the other kids with their parents filing into the room, the parents all shaking hands and smiling at each other. Only he and Randi had come alone.

Randi's parents wouldn't show up, of course. They'd be at work, probably, or else drinking somewhere. Jason wondered how they both managed to hold down jobs. Randi said they never got involved with her school projects or anything else. She'd told him a lot about them, how they argued and fought, and about the bruises her mother tried to hide . . . stuff like that. He could believe it. He'd never met her folks, but when he phoned her sometimes he could hear shouting in the background, and once her father had answered the phone and make some crack at him. Jason had hung up, not wanting to get Randi in trouble, but she'd called him back later, in tears, and told him it was another bad night at her house.

Randi wanted to run away—get a place of her

own—but she told him she felt kind of responsible for her little sister, Chrissie.

Jason looked around the big living room. This was some house Brad lived in! Everything clean and neat and comfortable. Jason remembered the furnished apartments he and Scott had lived in with their dad. It sure made a difference when there was a woman in the house. Shiny floors and windows, and flowers everywhere.

Brad was sitting on a window seat, his dad standing next to him, his mother at the door greeting the newcomers. Jenny Bradshaw was sitting next to a good-looking blonde woman who was an older version of Jenny; Tony and his father were on one of the couches; Peter—his dark, smooth hair neatly combed—with a well-dressed woman who was his mother; and little Dennis Wagstaff, who was only ten, sat between a worried-looking brunette and a tall guy with a beard.

Manny Bloom was coming through the front door now. Jason recognized his hearty voice. Mrs. Harris brought him in and introduced him all around. He smiled at everyone and shook hands. Jason noticed that he'd put on a different jacket for the occasion—this one just as worn out as the other one, but a bit cleaner. Randi must have noticed this too, because she poked Jason with her elbow and winked.

Manny perched on a piano bench and spoke to them. "I'm happy to meet all of you," he said. "You've got a talented bunch of kids here. We can be proud of all of them. They can earn money, and they can make the L.A. Wheels Skateboarding Team famous." There were a few nods and smiles, and some of the parents glanced fondly at their children.

Manny went on, "I've got the kids enthused about the idea, and I've got some backing to get the team started. Now all I need is your help and cooperation."

There were lots of questions. Tony's father wanted to know how far the team would be traveling, and Dennis's mother asked who would make sure the kids ate properly and got enough rest. Manny sounded reassuring. The team would go up and down the Pacific Coast, and he would see to it that everyone got three good meals and at least eight hours sleep a day. After all, they were athletes in training and would be treated like the professionals they were. Just let them get off to a good start and they could bring entertainment to thousands, as well as inspiration to other young people who might want to try the sport of skateboarding.

After an hour or so of questions and discussion, Manny distributed permission slips, the parents signed them, and the room emptied quickly until Randi and Jason were the only ones left, besides the Harrises.

They said good-bye and Manny walked outside with them. "What about you, Randi?" he asked her. "Don't your parents want to talk to me?"

She shook her head, the long, dark hair falling around her pretty face. "They said it was okay with them if it's okay with me."

"Yeah?" Manny looked at her suspiciously.

"It's cool," Jason told him, putting an arm around Randi's shoulders.

Manny pulled one of the slips from his pocket. "Just the same, you'll have to ask them to sign this. You're not eighteen yet, are you?"

Randi shook her head again, and took the slip.

"Well," Manny went on, "I wouldn't want to have them accusing me of kidnapping their daughter.."

Randi laughed.

"Okay, so it sounds funny," Manny said. "But it could happen."

"They don't care," Jason told him, holding Randi tightly. "They're too busy boozing it up."

A strange look crossed Manny's face for a moment. "Oh. Well, okay. Just get them to sign that slip."

He was still standing in the driveway, looking after them, as Jason helped Randi into the van and pulled away.

"What do you think of Manny?" Randi asked as she moved closer to him and rested her head on his arm.

"He seems like an all-right guy," Jason told her. "What do you think?"

"I don't know. He talks a lot. But maybe we *will* go on to fame and fortune this way, like he's always saying."

"Yeah," Jason said. "I can sure use the bread."

"Me too. But the part I like best is"—she cuddled closer—"that we'll be traveling together. We can be together every day, instead of like it is now."

"Right." It wouldn't be long until they gave their first show. Manny said he had some bookings lined up already.

Chapter 6

Our bus wasn't much to look at. All Manny could get was an old school bus with gray paint peeling off parts of it, coats of primer covering other parts, and some of it just bare metal; but we were just as happy as if it had been a limousine. We had our suitcases tied on the top of it, and we were all inside it ... the Los Angeles Wheels Skateboard Team, heading down the Pacific Coast Highway to our first performance, an auditorium in Oceanside.

"Hey, Manny!" I called to him. He was driving, and I was sitting in the seat across the aisle and just behind him. "How did you get us into this place, anyway?"

"Oceanside?" He grinned into his rear-view mirror at me. "Contacts, Brad. It's all in who you know!"

Jason, sitting across from me with Randi, shook his head. "Come on, Manny. Give it to us straight."

"Contacts, I told you. I know this guy in TV who put me on to it."

37

"We're going to be on TV?" Dennis whooped.

"Not exactly," Manny said. "He told me about this club in Oceanside. They like sports events, and every Saturday they go to one. This time they're coming to watch us."

"They pay a lot?" Randi asked.

"I'll worry about the finances," Manny told her. "You guys worry about the performance. Anyway, we can't start big. We've got to work up to it."

Dennis, on his skateboard, was trying some three-sixties, which wasn't easy on the moving bus.

"Please, Dennis," Manny said. "Come on. Don't practice on the bus."

Dennis didn't seem to hear. He tried a space walk down the center aisle. A spacewalk on a skateboard might not be as hard as walking on the moon but still it's not easy to keep your balance when you've got to keep both feet centered over the rear wheels of the board while the front of it is raised as high as you can get it. "I'm Luke Skywalker," he said. "I'm coming to save the princess!"

"Go sit down and save the princess!" Manny squawked at him.

Peter reached out a hand to stop Dennis as he passed. "Here, sit by me," he said. "I'll loan you my comic book."

I had brought my portable radio and set it on the seat beside me. I turned up the volume. There was a loud blast of music, Manny jumped nervously, and the bus swerved.

"Hey! Watch where you're going!" Peter called.

"Don't tell me how to drive," Manny said irritably. "I used to do this in the army."

"No wonder we lost the Civil War," Randi giggled.

Everyone laughed except Manny. "Brad, turn that thing down!"

"Okay, okay!" I like the Jefferson Starship, but it was kind of loud. I turned it down a notch.

"Hey, man," Tony called. "How much further?"

"A few more miles. Relax."

Randi grinned at Jason, nudged him, and leaned forward. "Hey, Manny! That group on the radio . . . I know one of the guys in it. Maybe they'd tour with us."

Manny glanced back at her over his shoulder. "Yeah? You know, they don't sound bad at all."

Jenny was cracking up, and I was afraid he'd hear her. The rest of us were having a hard time to keep from laughing, but Manny was taking it all seriously.

"That's a good idea," he went on. "You know, we could put together a combined concert and exhibition tour."

None of us could hold it in now; we all laughed, and Manny was mystified.

"What's so funny? What's the big joke?"

Tony finally told him. "Don't be such a lame goon, man. That's the Jefferson Starship! Don't you know anything?"

He didn't seem to. He was so square he didn't get it, and all he said was: "So?"

"Forget it," I told him. "They'd probably want a bigger bus."

When Manny finally understood the joke, he took it pretty well. "You couldn't prove it by me," he said. "Jefferson Starship, huh! I thought that was the name of our next space probe."

At the auditorium, he nosed the bus into a parking space and we all got out. We unloaded the suitcases containing our brand-new uniforms and followed Manny inside.

The place was big, but it wasn't crowded. Of course it was early yet. We wouldn't be starting for half an hour or so. Maybe the crowd would get bigger. Manny found out where the dressing rooms were so we could change, then led us down a dimly lit, narrow corridor.

Jenny and Randi went to the girls' dressing rooms on one side of the corridor, and the guys went into a room on the other side, Manny with us. He opened one of the suitcases and began handing out our new uniforms. We hadn't seen them before. They were these weird yellow-and-green jerseys with a spacey "L.A. Wheels" logo across the chest; short yellow pants, green and white knee socks, and green and white sneakers. When Manny gave these to us, I could tell it was going to be a problem to get everyone to wear them. It was hard enough to get the boys to wear shirts in the first place.

Jason looked at himself in a mirror, pulling a face. "You expect me to go out there in *this?*"

"What's the problem?" Manny asked him.

I knew what the problem was. I didn't like mine much either, and the other guys seemed to feel the same way. Maybe it was just because they looked strange at first. None of us had ever skated in uniforms before. Jeans and shirts were what we were used to.

Jason pulled his jersey off. "No way! I'm not wearing this."

"It looks terrific on you," Manny said, bewildered.

"It looks gay," Jason said.

We all followed Jason's lead. If he wouldn't wear it, we wouldn't. That's the effect Jason had on all of us. I took my jersey off and dropped it on the floor.

Manny was really having a fit. "Come on, you guys! It's all in your mind! They look great on you! It's the team uniform; you all have to wear it."

"Not me." Jason folded his arms across his bare chest.

Manny looked as though he might cry any minute. "Hey, come on! Those things cost plenty! Where would the Rams be without their uniforms! How about the Dodgers! Come on, we've got to look like a team!"

None of us said anything; we just watched Jason. But I thought Manny was right. Even if we felt strange in them at first, the bright green-and-yellow uniforms made us look like a professional team. I wouldn't say so, though. I'm not a top skater like Jason. Nobody would care what I thought.

Manny appealed to Jason once more. "If you wear yours, the rest of the guys will, too. Right, guys?"

Jason grinned suddenly. I guess he just didn't like to see Manny suffer. "Okay," he said. "I'll wear it. Just for you."

Manny's smile spread across his face. "You will? All right! Everybody put them back on. Okay, we're just about ready to roll."

We all trooped out to the auditorium and sat

down on the benches. The girls were already there waiting for us. Jenny looked pretty in her uniform, and Randi looked even better in hers than she had in her bikini, if that was possible. But as I looked around at the crowd, I couldn't believe it. There couldn't be more than thirty or forty people here, and it was time to start the show.

Manny was standing next to me, his face clouded. "Some opening night, huh?"

Randi came up to him. "You sure this is the right night?" she asked, being sarcastic.

"Very funny," Manny told her. "Well, we might as well start."

He walked to a platform at one end of the auditorium and picked up a microphone. "Testing . . . one, two, three." His words echoed over the empty seats, and he seemed to wince as the sound carried back to him. Then he put on a big, enthusiastic smile that came through in his voice. "Good evening, ladies and gentlemen. Welcome to the opening night of the Los Angeles Wheels' tour. Right now I'd like to introduce our first star attraction: the one, the only, the inimitable Peter, and we call him The Wolf, Steffens!"

Peter began with a barrel jump. After he warmed up with a few runs around the auditorium to pick up speed, he jumped the line of eight barrels neatly, and landed perfectly on the skateboard placed at the end of the line. There was applause and a few cheers. Peter built up speed again until he was going about ten miles an hour. He crouched, began a turn, and placed both hands on the ground as he came around. His hands helped him to pivot, breaking the traction of the skateboard wheels.

You could hear a sprinkling of applause as Manny's voice came wild and eager over the mike. "All right! How about that . . . what do you call it?"

"Power slide.!" We all shouted.

"Right. A power slide!"

Peter did some end-overs, with one foot on the tail of his board and the other on the nose, pivoting on the front wheels so that the tail swung around in a half-circle, then pivoting the rear wheels, so that the nose swung around. He continued the movements so that it seemed as if the board was walking itself. This trick has to be practiced a lot because unless your feet are placed exactly right, the board can flip over. Peter had it down perfectly, and the board moved around smoothly under his feet.

Then he got the board moving swiftly while he did a series of spinners, jumping up from the board and spinning his body in a complete circle, then landing in the same direction.

As he sat down, applause echoed through the auditorium. Even though the crowd was sparse, they really appreciated our show.

"And now," Manny said, "I have somebody I'd like you to meet, somebody who's going to go on to bigger and better things on the skateboard horizon. One of our female members, one of our stellar attractions, let's give a rousing welcome to pretty Jenny Bradshaw!"

There was more applause for Jenny as she skated to the center of the auditorium. Someone had started music and the rhythm of it pulsed around the half-empty place as Jenny put her hands on each end of the skateboard and went into a handstand, picking up momentum as she arched her back and brought her legs up into position above her head.

The audience cheered for her, and the rest of the team did, too. She had a fluid grace that was impressive. Jenny dropped out of the handstand position and got one foot on her skateboard, pushing it along with the other foot. Then she put that foot on the board and moved the back foot ahead of it, walking on her skateboard.

One of her specialties is the daffy, which depends on knowing how to do nose and tail wheelies expertly. Jenny did a nose wheelie first, then a tail wheelie, then, with two skateboards, she did a nose wheelie on the back foot and a tail wheelie on the front foot. The crowd loved the daffy, so Jenny did a two-board nose wheelie for an encore.

Randi was introduced, and she crouched in Jenny's path so Jenny could skate up to her, jump over her body, and land on the skateboard that was waiting on the other side. Then Randi went into her freestyle maneuvers as Jenny went back to the bench.

Dennis was on next, and the crowd loved him. They seemed amazed to see how that little towheaded ten year old could handle a skateboard. He skated around the auditorium, got up to a comfortable speed, put his left foot on the center of the board, and crouched, extending his other leg out in front of him in the christie. Then he did the coffin for them, and they loved that, too. He lay on his back on his moving skateboard, and folded his hands together over his chest.

He ended his performance with a series of three-sixties, getting his right foot over the tail of the board so that the front wheels lifted, then twisting his body hard to the left so that the whole board made a complete rotation. He made it look so easy; I bet most of the crowd thought they could do it if they only had skateboards under their feet.

When it was my turn to go out there, I felt an electric thrill in the pit of my stomach. People were applauding for me, and I hoped I could make them clap even harder when I was through, but this was the first time I'd ever performed for anybody, and I was nervous. I started off with some spinners, went into some one foot nose three-sixties and some handstand wheelies, which are the same as nose and tail wheelies except you do them standing on your hands. I finished up with a Y. I got my board going backwards at a good speed, lifted my leg straight up and grabbed my foot with my hand, then lifted my other arm to make a "Y" position of my body.

Cheers and applause rose from the crowd, and I suddenly noticed that I hadn't been nervous at all once I started skateboarding. I'd been too busy concentrating on what I was doing.

As I sat down, Tony took his turn and then, after him, came Jason.

Manny really made a production out of introducing him. "I'd like to introduce to you the racing phenomenon, the California Downhill Skateboarding Champion. Since we didn't bring a hill with us, he'll do some freestyle for you. The one, the only . . . Jason Maddox!"

I watched Jason go into an incredible series of freestyle tricks. He raced around the auditorium, did a handstand at high speed and then went into an L-sit which he did by centering himself on the

moving skateboard and putting his hands on the
ends of the board, then lifting his body off the
board and extending his legs forward so that his
whole body formed an "L." From there, he
brought his legs upward and together, to make a V-
sit position.

He did a lot of the same things the rest of us had
done, but I could see that he had a style and an
easy confidence that made a lot of difference. The
people were really going wild for him. I knew I
could never be that good. There was no argument.
Jason was the best.

Chapter 7

When the show was over and the kids had gone to their dressing rooms to change, Manny felt his good spirits falling fast. The turnout for their first performance had been pretty sad, and the money wasn't enough to cover their first day's meals and motel bill. He'd have to find a motel that wasn't too expensive, to keep the costs down. The money Sol gave him had to stretch, at least until they could see some profits.

When the kids got back on the bus, he kept his face cheerful. There was no use getting them worried. They'd done a great job, every one of them.

He drove the bus along the coast highway, hearing the kids talking quietly in the back, discussing the show they'd put on. He'd noticed that Randi and Jason always sat close together. Now they were in one of the back seats. He wasn't arguing against young love, but he had to think about the reaction on the other kids, and the parents, who expected him to keep their kids happy, healthy, and out of trouble. He was trying to think of some

47

excuse to get both of them up to the front of the bus with everybody else, when he saw a neon sign on the beach up ahead. Some of the letters had burned out, so it read OCE N FRONT OTEL —VACAN Y. In the moonlight the motel looked like a middle-aged, weatherbeaten group of buildings huddled under a couple of palm trees, but it *didn't* look expensive, and that was good. Manny pulled into the driveway in front of it.

"This looks like our place for tonight," he told the kids. "Wait here while I check it out." He left the bus and went up to a closed door with "Office" printed on its dark window.

Manny tapped on the glass two or three times before he heard a woman's voice inside bawling: "Hold on! I'm coming!" Then lights went on behind the glass and the door opened a crack.

The woman was fat and wore a grimy bathrobe. She looked sleepy. "Waddya want?"

"Do you have any rooms available?" Manny asked her.

The woman shook her head in disgust and pointed to the VACAN Y sign flashing on and off.

"No," she said sarcastically. "I just leave the sign on because the electric company needs the money."

Manny managed to keep the smile on his face. "Do you have four rooms?"

The woman looked suspicious. "I don't hold with no wild parties."

"Look, lady, I'm the owner of the Los Angeles Wheels. My team's out there in the bus. They're all kids."

The woman opened the door a little wider and

squinted out into the night. "The Los Angeles what?"

"Wheels. The Los Angeles Wheels. The professional skateboard team."

'If they've got skateboards, why do they need a bus?" The woman cackled at her own joke.

"It's getting late, lady," Manny said. "The team's tired. You want to make some money or not?"

The woman opened the door to admit him, then went around a counter and pulled several blank cards out of a drawer. "Fill out a separate registration card for each room. It's fifteen a room . . . in advance."

Manny reached into his back pocket and pulled out a checkbook. "Who do I make this out to?"

The woman sneered and pointed to a sign that read "Cash Only Accepted." "Can't you read?" she asked him.

Manny shuddered. "Cash?"

"Cash," the woman said flatly.

Manny pulled out some bills, counted out sixty dollars, and placed the money on the counter.

"Plus room tax," the woman said.

He looked unhappily at what was left. One bill and some loose change. "You've left me with no cash," he told the woman.

She eyed his round body. "You won't starve to death," she said. "Here are your keys."

There were four of them, each one numbered.

The woman pointed out four cabins joined together, fronting on the beach, with a wooden walkway stretching in front of them that ran the length of the building.

Manny led his team to them. "Randi and Jenny can share this first one," he said as he found the key to open the rickety, peeling door.

Randi wrinkled her nose as she entered the cabin. "Smells like their last tenant died and was buried in here."

Jenny bounced on one of the beds. "Looks okay to me, Randi. And we're right on the beach. We can hear the ocean all night!"

Randi sat gingerly on the edge of the other bed. "For sure we'll have to leave the window open all night so we can breathe."

"Cheer up," Manny told her. "We'll all go for a swim in the morning."

Leaving Randi and Jenny, the boys went on down the walkway to the next door, following Manny. He opened the door to let them in, and then he noticed Jason wasn't with them. He let the other boys go inside while he went back to the first cabin.

Randi and Jason were standing in the doorway, their arms around each other, kissing.

"Make it short, Jason," Manny said, and went back to the next cabin.

The room wasn't much—a double bed and a single, both covered with worn-out faded cotton bedspreads; a ravelling rug over the exact center of the wooden floor; a tiny bathroom; a picture of the Grand Canyon on one wall. *Not too cheerful,* he thought. Not exactly the lap of luxury, but it would do for tonight. "I'll take this room," he said. "Dennis, do you want to sleep in the other bed over there?"

Dennis chewed his gum thoughtfully, his head on one side.

"Maybe you'd rather bunk in with Brad and me," Peter suggested.

Dennis seemed to like that idea better. That was good, Manny thought. Peter was treating Dennis like a kid brother, and Manny admired that quality in him.

"Good idea," Manny told them, noting that Jason had slipped quietly into the room as they talked. "Jason, you and Tony can have the room next to this one, and we'll put you other three in the last one."

When he'd got them all settled in for the night, Manny stretched out on his bed, fully clothed, and turned on his bed lamp. He'd taken a can of Mountain Dew out of the styrofoam cooler in the bus, and now he opened a paperback and read as he sipped the drink, his ears tuned to any footsteps outside his window. He wasn't going to go for anybody sneaking around outside, or if the guys got the idea for an unauthorized midnight swim, he wanted to know about it. He could hear the murmur of the kids' voices on either side of him—the four cabins shared common walls—and he read with only half his attention on the book until the sounds from the other rooms quieted down at last.

Next morning, early, the kids were all up and into the ocean for a swim. Manny sat on the sand and watched them for a while. When he saw Randi coming out of the water, he sauntered toward her room, giving her enough time to change before he tapped on her door.

"Can I see you a minute?" he asked as she opened it.

She looked worried. "What's up?"

"I just want to talk with you," Manny said easily. "Jenny still in the water?"

The girl nodded.

"Then we can talk a few minutes alone." He closed the door behind him and sat down in a chair beside the window.

Randi, wearing blue shorts and a T-shirt, her wet hair tied back with a kerchief, sat uneasily on the edge of the bed. "What do you want?"

"Don't look so worried. This won't take long. Just a little private talk, that's all." He felt embarrassed, and he was just as uncomfortable as she was, but he had to do this, he knew. He had to keep these kids out of trouble, and the parents happy. He smiled, hoping it would make her feel more at ease. "Tell me," he said. "Are you enjoying yourself on the team?"

"Sure. It keeps me in shape."

"It's tough to keep in shape, huh?"

Randi eyed him. "Yeah. Especially for some people."

Manny got her inference, but he ignored it. She was always putting him down, and he wondered why. Maybe she just didn't like him. Well, she wasn't going to like him much better after this, but that couldn't be helped. The team was what counted. "How old are you, Randi?" he asked. "Seventeen?"

"I'll be eighteen in August."

"You always watch what you eat and get plenty of sleep?"

She nodded. "Yeah. So?"

"So what time were you in bed last night?"

She looked down at her hands folded in her lap. "I don't know. Twelve-thirty . . . one."

The lie made him angry. "That's not true!"

She looked up at him, her face reddening. "You mind explaining that remark?"

"I know you weren't in bed at twelve-thirty or one o'clock."

"I was too."

"Yeah? Well, you might have been in bed, but you weren't asleep."

Randi jumped up and glared down at him. "Just who do you think you are . . . my father?"

Manny tried to keep his voice calm. "No. But I'll tell you who I am. I'm the manager of this team, and I'm responsible for all the fourteen and fifteen and seventeen-going-on-eighteen year olds. I've even got a ten year old on this team, Randi. What do you think the parents are going to do if they find out you kids are taking advantage of your freedom?"

"What do you mean?"

"You and Jason, Miss Innocent. You and Jason. What do you think, I'm blind to what's going on. . ."

Randi headed for the door. "I don't have to listen to this," she said.

"Where are you going?"

"For some fresh air," she said, turning at the doorway. "Does that meet with your approval?"

"Randi, listen! All I'm asking you to do is to cool it while we're on the road. What you do back in Los Angeles is your own business."

She only glared at him and went out, slamming the door behind her. Manny sighed. It had been just as bad as he'd feared. Now she hated him, probably, and maybe she'd get Jason mad at him too. Well, it couldn't be helped, but for a while he wished that he *was* her father. Poor kid, believing her parents didn't care what she did, she must feel that Jason was the only one in the world who could love her and care about her. Manny just couldn't believe it.

He got up slowly, shaking his head, and went out of the cabin. If I were her father, he mused, I'd be so proud of her beauty and talents. I'd talk to her and be interested in everything she did. Some parents are so darn short-sighted. They figure once their kids get past the diaper and oatmeal stage they can take care of themselves. Actually, I think the parents want to take care of THEMSELVES. Don't they know that teen-age girls are as sensitive as birds and need as much TLC as they can get. Maybe the parents need to grow up.

Chapter 8

The Los Angeles Wheels traveled to San Diego to put on a show in an arena there; they performed in a park in Santa Ana and one in Santa Barbara. In Bakersfield they did a good show in an empty swimming pool in a city park; in Fresno they set up a show around two big drainage pipes. The Wheels visited cities as far north as Chico and as far south as Coronado, but still they hadn't made quite as much money as they'd hoped for, and the big crowds just weren't coming to see them.

Manny was worried. Sol's money was dwindling, and he hadn't yet been able to pay the kids anything. It was a simple matter of bookkeeping—the expenses were bigger than the profits.

When they landed home again for a few days' rest, Manny decided he was going to do nothing but stay in his apartment and sleep for twenty-four hours. Traveling with a bunch of teen-agers was pretty hectic. There was constantly something to look after. Dennis was always losing his knee pads or gloves and half the time Tony forgot his uniform. One time he even had to drive fifty miles back to the motel where Jenny left her suitcase. The music on the bus was turned up so high he thought for sure he'd lost his hearing in his left ear. And oh, God, they were always hungry or had to go to the bathroom. At thirty-three, Manny felt as though he were pushing ninety.

But he had just closed his eyes when the phone rang. He forced himself to answer it. Who could tell? It might be good news.

"Hello. E.B.A.," he said in his secretary's voice.

"Manny, what did I tell you about that falsetto?" Sol's voice thundered over the phone.

"Oh. Hi, Sol. Sorry. I didn't know it was you."

"I'm disappointed, Manny."

"Disappointed? About what?"

Sol's voice became lower and more threatening. "Nobody's going to your shows. I'm worried about my investment."

"These things take a while, Sol."

Sol ignored his explanation. "You know what happens when I get worried about my investments?"

Manny's hands began to shake. "No. What?"

"Everybody involved with me gets worried about their health," Sol said. "Are you worried about your health, Manny?"

"I'm *terrified* about my health."

"Good. You should be." The phone at Sol's end clicked.

Manny sat holding the dead phone, wishing he

hadn't answered it. He knew Sol was capable of a lot of things—none of them good—if he didn't at least get his money back.

He crawled under the bedcovers, but now his eyes wouldn't close. He kept hearing Sol's voice on the phone, low and threatening.

It must have been the unluckiest day of his life, that first day he met Sol. That had been how long ago . . . three years? Yeah, it was just after he got married.

Manny had been doing all right then. He had a few really good clients who were bringing in enough money for him to live pretty well. There was that singer, Thursday Blue was her professional name, and an actress, Ginger Keen . . . a few like them. He'd get bookings for them in nightclubs, movies, TV, and take ten percent of their earnings. Business was getting better and better, and prospects really looked good. He got six weeks in Las Vegas for Thursday Blue, and Ginger was all set for a starring role in a movie.

Then he'd married Celia.

Celia had been another one of his clients. Not much talent, but with beauty and charm enough to take her anywhere she wanted to go. She wanted to go with Manny. Trouble was, she also wanted to go first class, even to the grocery store, and Manny wasn't earning quite enough money to satisfy all her expensive tastes.

He'd tried, though. For a wedding present he'd spent a year's earnings on a mink coat, and after the honeymoon he'd bought her a Jaguar. They had a beach house at Malibu as well as an apartment in Beverly Hills, and Celia opened charge accounts in all the best stores.

It hadn't taken more than a few months of high living before Manny realized he couldn't keep it up. They had to cut back expenses or go broke.

Celia made a big scene when he suggested economizing. She cried and said she didn't have to live like a pauper, and she wouldn't stay with him if he was going to be stingy with her. The solution she came up with was very simple, she told him. All he had to do was make more money.

Well, Manny tried that too, but the money just didn't come in fast enough. He took to gambling—horses, cards, football games—anything that might bring in more fast bread. But he'd never been a lucky gambler, and his desperation didn't help. He lost at everything.

Then one of his friends introduced him to Sol. Sol was a gambler too, but a lucky one. Not only would he take bets, he'd loan Manny money to make the bets. Manny borrowed money from Sol and lost bets with monotonous regularity. His clients began to feel he was neglecting them; since Manny was spending so much time gambling he had none to spare for them, and they drifted away, one by one, to other agents until Manny's business hit bottom.

Manny owed Sol thousands by that time. Every once in a while he'd get a lucky streak, and the money would flow back into Sol's pockets to pay back what he owed. Celia found out the stores wouldn't honor her charge account cards until their bills were paid, and the landlord was coming around to ask for the back rent. She decided this wasn't the kind of life she wanted, so she split.

That was okay. It hurt Manny to find out she didn't want to stick with him through his troubles, but by that time he realized he didn't love her very much either. She was like cotton candy—all pink and pretty on the outside, but nothing much on the inside, and she'd left a sickeningly sweet taste in his mouth. When her lawyer told him he'd have to give her monthly alimony, he figured it was a small price to pay to be rid of her.

Sol worried him a lot more than Celia did. Sol was a dangerous man. Sol loved a dollar better than he loved his right hand, and Sol wasn't going to let go of Manny until he'd paid off every nickel he owed him. Sol had tough friends who could kill if they thought that was what Sol wanted.

After the divorce, Manny moved into a cheap apartment and let his secretary go, cutting expenses down as far as he could, but his business had been dead for too long. All the clients he could find were amateurs or untalented hopefuls. Sol kept track of every move he made, and tonight, on the phone, it sounded as though his patience was getting desperately thin. Manny was indeed worried about his health suffering if he couldn't pay off Sol.

The L.A. Wheels was his only hope now. It was insane that his life depended on the erratic psyches and energies of seven kids. He couldn't even let them know, these carefree California skateboarders, that his very life (or death) depended on them. The best he could do was to work with them, pace them, keep them up so they didn't get too bored and bug off. He would have to try and not pressure them. He was walking a tightrope and felt like that guy who climbed the World Trade Center

Building in New York—like a human fly. He would either fly free or be swatted down. If they didn't come through, Manny might end up in a hospital or even a morgue.

Manny didn't get much sleep that night after all.

Chapter 9

We were playing the San Diego Civic Auditorium that night. Filing out of our bus, wearing the team's new green jackets, all of us were excited about giving our show in such a big place.

"Isn't this a trip?" Jenny said, walking beside me. "Getting paid to skate?"

"It'll be okay if Fatso doesn't eat up all the profits," Randi said.

"Who's getting paid?" Jason asked. "I haven't seen any bread yet."

"Me either." I shifted my Nike bag from one hand to the other and reached into my back pocket. My folks had given me ten dollars spending money, and I wanted to be sure it was still there. It was.

The auditorium was less than half full. We tried not to feel disappointed. The crowds were still staying away, but Manny kept telling us we had to build up a reputation first. These things came slowly. Word had to have time to get around to people. Besides, exhibition skateboarding was so new a sport that lots of people didn't know how exciting it could be. After all, it took a famous athlete like Pele to put soccer on the map in the U.S. Maybe the L.A. Wheels can do the same with skate-boarding.

They'd set up ramps in the auditorium—wooden ramps on both sides to make a half pipe, and a long ramp at one end where we could set up slalom cones.

We were all in good form that night. Jenny and Randi went out first to do their freestyle routines, doing handstands and wheelies. Then Randi performed the bunny-hop. She got up some speed on her board and crouched, getting one foot on the tail of the board and the other on the nose. She got a hand wrapped around each foot, grasping each end of the board at the same time, then lifted the board off the ground in a hopping motion.

While Randi bunny-hopped, Jenny did some ballet on the skateboard. She did a royal christie, crouching on her board and extending one leg to the side and her arms to the other side, then went into an arabesque, standing, her left leg held out gracefully behind her as she leaned forward, arms outstretched. The audience loved it, and both girls got a lot of applause.

Manny was talking them up over the microphone. "Randi Peterson, doing her famous bunny-hop. How about that! Let's hear it for Randi. And there's Jenny Bradshaw. A big hand for the ladies of the Los Angeles Wheels!"

Then the guys came out.

We slalomed down the long ramp and went down the center, between the two side ramps, skating up the sides, doing a kick turn at the top, and then down and up the other side, like skating in a drainpipe. Then while Dennis, Jason, and I continued to ride the ramps, Tony and Peter raced to the other end of the auditorium where a bar had been set across two poles, and began jumping over it, sending their skateboards under it and landing on them as they came down.

Manny talked all through our performance. "There's Peter the Wolf. Airborne, as usual. Go, Tony! That's a high bar, folks. The L.A. Wheels special high jump. That ramp the guys are climbing is ten feet high, folks. The angle is about fifty-five degrees!"

Applause scattered through the crowd, cheering us on. The music blared out a throbbing rhythm. We all loved skateboarding, and the thrill hit me even here in front of all these people, with all the commotion around me. Each time I hit the top of a ramp I got that special feeling of hanging weightless, suspended in time and space. For a second I wasn't in the world, but out somewhere on my own where no one could ever be with me. It was like no other sensation I'd ever known—a total rush, Tony called it—and that was it for me, too. It felt good, knowing my body could move just right to make the skateboard do what I wanted it to, and the skills I'd acquired through hours and hours of practice made the board as much a part of me as my feet, to obey every movement of my muscles and nerves. I was building up to my big moment of the night . . . a trick I'd done only a couple of times before.

"And now, here's something really special,"

Manny announced as the music stopped and the other kids went back to the benches. "Here's something most of you have never seen before. Brad Harris will now attempt to jump over nine barrels. You heard me . . . nine! Come on out, Brad."

Feeling good, feeling great, I watched the barrels being set up for me as I circled the auditorium, building up speed. The audience was hushed, the whole place quiet. I'd seen Jason and Tony both do barrel jumps before. Now I was finally getting my chance.

The men got the barrels in place and I made another circle to gather the momentum I'd need. When I approached the barrels, I was going mighty fast.

I could see the first one right in front of my skateboard. I leaped, staying as low as I dared to, clearing the first few barrels that passed in a blur under me, tensing my body to stretch over all of them. But I'd made the jump too low, and I began to drop too soon. There was the last barrel directly under me, and I was going to land right on it!

The impact jolted me upwards and sideways at the same time. I closed my eyes and felt my body crushed on the floor as it landed, and a stabbing pain going through my shoulder.

For a time there was nothing but blackness and then, after what seemed to be a long silence, I became aware of the sounds of rolling wheels and anxious voices.

Someone was bending over me, her voice in my ear. Jenny . . . calling my name. "Brad! Can you hear me? Are you okay?"

I tried to answer, but my voice didn't seem to

work. I could hear other voices, and Manny shouting: "Don't touch him! Don't try to move him! Give him some air!"

"Is it your head?" Jenny asked, still close to me.

Finally my words came out. "My shoulder."

Jason's voice, angry, "I told you, Manny. Nine barrels was too many."

"All right, how was I supposed to know? I thought he could do it, okay?" Manny sounded uptight. Then he shouted. "Anybody here know first aid?"

"Call a doctor." Jason's voice again.

Manny. "That's it, a doctor." His voice lowered for a few seconds, then I could hear him speaking over the mike. "Just a little mishap, folks. Nothing to worry about. Please don't panic. Just stay where you are. The show will continue in just a few minutes."

I could open my eyes now, and I saw the team standing around me looking worried. Jenny stayed kneeling beside me, and in a short time some men in white came toward me with a stretcher, and put me on a wheeled cart. Manny and Jenny came with me in the ambulance.

At the hospital, a doctor examined me thoroughly and said I was lucky, it was only a sprain and a couple of nasty bruises. He put my arm in a sling and gave me an aspirin to take away the pain. When he finally let me get out of there, it was late. Manny and Jenny walked with me out to the parking lot, and we could see the hulk of the old bus there in the darkness. Jason must have driven it to the hospital, and he and the others were all waiting inside.

Manny helped me up the steps. "You sit right behind me and relax," he told me, taking the driver's seat and starting the motor.

Most of the kids were asleep. Jason was stretched out on the seat behind me, and Randi had settled next to him. When Manny started the engine it must have wakened both of them because Jason tapped me on my good shoulder. I turned around to see him sitting up, stretching.

"How'd it go, Brad?"

"Okay. I'm okay. Nothing serious."

Jenny took the seat across the aisle from me. "The doctor said he was lucky. It's only a sprain that should heal in a few days."

Jason grinned at me. "When word gets around what happened to you tonight, maybe the crowds will get bigger. They'll come to watch us break our necks."

Randi laughed and so did Jenny.

I didn't feel like laughing. "I shouldn't have tried your trick, Jason. I should have left that to you guys who can do it right." Somehow I felt as though I had to apologize. Maybe because out there in the auditorium, just before the jump, I'd thought I could do anything.

"You can do it, Brad. Accidents can happen to anybody." Jason seemed embarrassed.

"No. You wouldn't have fouled it up like I did."

He shook his head, then leaned back with his arm around Randi and closed his eyes again.

I watched out the window as the bus drove homeward through the darkness. I couldn't see much except stars hanging low over the empty stretches of desert, and now and then the lights from the little towns we passed. I felt ashamed of the accident. There was no way I could ever be as good as Jason. I shouldn't even have tried.

It was very early in the morning when we got home, the first pale light of dawn showing faintly on the horizon. Manny told the others he wanted to get me home right away, so we stopped at my house first.

Every room in the house was lit. You could see the lights from the driveway. I knew my folks must have been worried. Manny told me he'd phoned them from the hospital.

Sure enough, they were waiting on the front porch as Manny and I got out of the bus. They couldn't wait to see for themselves that I was okay.

"I'll be right back after I talk to Brad's folks," Manny told the rest of the team. "Just sit tight."

My dad called to us. "You all right, son?"

"Sure."

"It's only a sprain," Manny said as we climbed the steps and they led us inside, but he was nervous, I could tell. Probably worried about what they were going to say to him.

My mom inspected my bandage. "What did the doctor say?" she asked.

"He said I'll be fine in a few days, Mom."

"Do you need an aspirin, Brad? Are you in pain or anything?" She didn't look as though she believed I'd be okay.

I tried to calm her. "The doctor already gave me aspirin to take away the pain. I don't feel any pain. I'll be fine."

My dad went into the living room. "Will you come in and sit down for a minute, Mr. Bloom?"

Manny sat down and looked uncomfortable. "Manny—call me Manny. I'm sorry this happened, Mr. Harris. As I told you on the phone, these accidents can happen."

I wanted to hear what was going on, so I went into the living room and sat on the couch. Mom sat down beside me and plumped up a pillow to put behind me.

Dad went on talking. "It's not necessary to apologize," he told Manny, "but my wife and I have been talking things over."

I caught my breath. They weren't going to say I couldn't be on the team, were they?

Manny checked his watch anxiously. "The others are waiting on the bus outside, Mr. Harris, and they're all tired."

"This won't take long."

"Can I get you a drink?" my mom asked Manny.

"No thanks." He glanced through the window at the bus.

"You see," Mom said, "we had Brad late in life. He's our only child."

"We try not to be overprotective," Dad said.

"But we do have some concerns," Mom added.

Manny took a handful of nuts from a bowl on the table near his chair. I squirmed, waiting for what might be coming, knowing I was going to argue if they tried to make me quit the team. I knew that Dad, especially, thought skateboarding was dangerous. I knew he didn't really like it when I spent a lot of time at it. I kept quiet, waiting to hear what they had to say.

Mom was talking now. "I know many parents today let their kids do whatever they want. We're probably old-fashioned, but we feel there has to be some kind of supervision besides yourself."

Manny took another handful of nuts. "I understand your concern, and I want you to know . . ." he hesitated, chewing thoughtfully, ". . . that I'm getting a complete first-aid kit for the team."

Dad shook his head. "It's not just the medical aspect."

"I thought that's what we were talking about," Manny said.

Mom frowned. "Not entirely. Take the Bradshaw girl . . . Jenny? She's fourteen. And that little Wagstaff boy is only ten."

"Kids know a lot more today than we did at their age," Dad said.

"You're not married, are you?" Mom asked.

"Not at the moment, no." Manny saw the bowl of pretzels that sat beside the nuts, and helped himself to some of those. "The kids seem to be having a good time on the team," he said, sounding helpless.

"That's why we want it to work out," Mom said. "I just somehow think you need some more supervision for the children. A woman, for instance."

Manny seemed to be choking on the pretzel, his face turning red. "Female supervision? You mean a woman traveling with us?"

Dad nodded, and I almost laughed with relief. They weren't going to ask me to leave the team after all!

"Why don't you think about our suggestion?" Dad asked Manny.

Manny stood up quickly. "All right, I'll do that.

We'll work something out."

Dad went with him to the door, and I got up, ready to go to bed. I didn't think Manny liked their idea too well. I wondered what he was going to do about it.

Chapter 10

The next afternoon Manny went through the classified section of the *Times*. There was no way he was going to get out of doing what the Harrises wanted. They had probably talked to the other parents, and the last thing he wanted was to have the parents down on him about anything. Sitting at his desk in the living room, a half-empty box of donuts and a Mountain Dew beside him, he read the "Jobs Wanted" column.

There was one ad that looked like what he wanted, and he pulled a pen from his shirt pocket and circled it. "Registered nurse seeks interesting employment. Will travel. 656-6565." He assumed the nurse was female, and a woman who was also a nurse would be ideal. He picked up the phone and dialed the number.

A woman with a tired, nasal voice answered the phone. "Hello?"

"I'm calling about the ad you placed in today's *Times*."

"Yes?"

"I'm Emanuel Bloom, the owner of the Los Angeles Wheels."

"The Los Angeles what?"

"Wheels. The Los Angeles Wheels professional skateboard team."

"Never heard of them. This woman had the most unattractive voice he'd ever heard. She sounded bitter, middle-aged, and bad-tempered, and he almost hung up on her until he remembered there had been only one ad in the column that might do, and he needed someone fast. Besides, he'd bet a woman like this could handle anything, and wasn't that what he needed?

He explained patiently. "That's because we've just started up and we need a nurse. I was wondering if you'd be interested?"

"What's it pay?" the voice asked.

Manny looked at the box of donuts, hesitated, and then took one. "The salary would, of course, depend upon your experience and—"

"I need two hundred dollars a week," she interrupted.

Manny shut his eyes and felt a pain in his wallet. "How about one seventy-five?"

"Look," the woman said flatly. "I need a job and you apparently need a nurse. A hundred and eighty-seven fifty."

Manny mopped his forehead with the sleeve of his shirt. "Fine. Can you start right away?"

"Sure."

"We should meet first and discuss the details. How about the Melting Pot restaurant tomorrow at noon?"

"Okay."

"Oh, and your name is Nurse . . . ?"

"Broderick. Millicent Broderick."

"Of course you've worked with professional athletes before?"

"I was the traveling nurse for the Cleveland Browns."

Manny had a picture of her in his mind as he sat in the Melting Pot, waiting. She would be severely dressed, with her hair pulled back in a tidy bun, and she would probably weigh more than he did. He pulled a breadstick from a basket in front of him and munched on it as he looked over the crowd of diners for someone to match that description. There was no one. Impatiently, he glanced at his watch, then signaled the maitre d'.

"I'm Mr. Bloom. Are you sure someone hasn't asked for me?"

"Yes, I'm sure, Mr. Bloom."

Manny took another breadstick. "Okay, thanks."

A couple came in and were shown to a table. The woman looked like his mind-picture of Millicent Broderick, but she didn't seem to be searching for him. She and her companion sat down, picked up their menus, and studied them.

A pretty, dark-haired woman in jeans and a T-shirt walked past his table. Manny watched her admiringly as she walked over to the maitre d', talked with him a moment, then turned toward Manny.

This lovely thing was Millicent Broderick? Manny couldn't believe his eyes.

"Mr. Bloom?" she asked, sounding not at all like the voice on the phone.

"I'm Emanuel Bloom," Manny managed to say.

She leaned over the table and extended her hand.

"Hi. I'm Broderick."

"No, you're not," Manny said.

"Excuse me?"

"I talked to Millicent Broderick on the phone yesterday and it wasn't you." Manny said. "She was old, nasally, and ugly."

"That's exactly how I felt when I talked to you."

Manny pointed to the chair at the other side of the table. "Sit down."

She lowered her body gracefully into the chair while Manny eyed her appreciatively.

She must have noticed. She smiled. "I'm sorry. Maybe I should have worn my uniform. I look lots more businesslike in it."

Manny looked at his watch. "You're almost half an hour late. Didn't the Browns teach you to be on time?"

She shook her head, her long, dark hair bouncing. "I'm usually late on the first day of a job."

"That's not so good."

She smiled at him. "It's better than the second day. I don't usually show up then at all."

Manny sighed. "Another smart mouth I don't need, lady. I've got seven of them on my team already."

She looked contrite. "I'm sorry. I really *can* be on time, and I will. That is, if I get the job."

"Let's exchange some information and see." Manny picked another breadstick out of the basket. "Why did you quit the Browns?"

She shrugged. "I wanted to move away from Cleveland, so I came here to Los Angeles."

Manny saw a waiter coming toward them. "Would you like something?" he asked Millicent.

"No thanks. I've already eaten."

"Then how about a glass of wine?"

"That sounds fine. Chianti would be great."

Manny ordered wine and spaghetti from the waiter, then turned his attention back to Millicent. "How did you become a team nurse?"

"Well . . . I've never been any good at typing." She laughed, then became suddenly serious as she looked at Manny's face. "Sorry. I'll try to remember about the smart mouth. Okay . . . back in Canton, Ohio, where I went to school, I decided I wanted to spend my life doing something worthwhile. You know, use my education to help people. Nursing seemed like the best answer, so I got my R.N. there. Since I also like to travel, I found a spot with the Browns. It's more fun than working regular shifts in a hospital."

"But you didn't enjoy it much after you tried it?" Manny liked the fact that she wanted to help people, but he wondered about her wanting to travel so much. He didn't want to hire her and then have her travel on somewhere else when he needed her.

"I loved every minute of it," Millicent said. She hesitated for a moment, looking uncomfortable, before she went on. "But there was a guy on the team . . . we had a thing going for each other for a while. Then I found out he was married. There wasn't much else I could do except get away from him and the Browns and Cleveland as fast as possible." She looked down at her fingers that were tracing the edge of her napkin on the table top.

Manny could understand. He had seen the pain in her eyes . . . on her face . . . as she talked about it, and he felt sympathy for her. He knew what impossible situations love could get you into. He *should* know.

"I have to ask you questions like that," he said softly. "You know. I've got to be sure you're the right person for us."

She nodded silently. Manny was glad that the waiter chose that moment to come and place the food and wine in front of them. He busied himself with a forkful of spaghetti until Millicent looked more composed.

"Tell me about the Los Angeles Wheels," she said. "Who are they, and what does a skateboard team actually do?"

"You ever see roller derby or the Ice Capades?"

She nodded.

"Well, we do something like that. We travel up and down the coast, putting on exhibitions of skateboarding. We're going to be so big some day that nobody will have to ask who we are!"

She was smiling now, and Manny felt good.

"And how old are the kids?" she asked. "They *are* kids?"

"Yeah, they're all kids. The oldest—he's eighteen—is Jason Maddox. He's the best skater I've got. But there's a problem with him because he's involved with this seventeen-year-old girl who's also on the team. He talked me into putting her on the team, too." He took a sip of water. "You understand what I'm saying?"

She nodded. "Yeah, I see."

"Then our youngest one is ten . . . a little kid named Dennis. He *thinks* he's eighteen. And Brad Harris, he almost broke his shoulder going over nine barrels the other night."

"Almost broke it? Is he okay now?"

"It turned out to be a sprain. He's healing up pretty fast. But, you see, I need a combination nurse and mother, sort of. Can you see what I mean?"

"With a team of teen-agers? Yeah, I can. And I know I can fill the job. Okay?"

Manny smiled. "Okay."

"A hundred and eighty-seven fifty, right?"

"Right."

"Here's to the Los Angeles Wheels!" Millicent lifted her wineglass.

Manny clicked his water glass against it. "And to their new nurse," he said.

Chapter 11

Our first competition skating came about the same time my shoulder healed. We were to skate under the lights against the El Tigres team at the Torrance Skater Cross Skateboard Park. We had more of a crowd than we'd ever had, although the grandstands were still only half-filled. We were all looking forward to the competition, though. As Manny pointed out, it added a lot more excitement to our show.

Jenny and I were sitting together on one of the benches before the game, checking out skateboards to make sure the wheel locknuts and hanger plate mounting nuts were tight enough. The last thing any skater wants is a board that's not in perfect condition. We can get up to some pretty good speeds on them, and the skateboards really take a beating, so we check them before and after each performance. If anything's wrong that we can't fix, we use another board.

"What do you think of the new team nurse?" I asked Jenny.

She looked over at Millicent, standing talking to Manny. "She seems to be pretty neat to talk to. Do you like her?"

"She's real foxy," I said, leering.

"I don't think Manny's noticed," Jenny said. "He's all business with her."

The announcer's voice cut into our conversation. "Ladies and gentlemen, the bank riding competition will begin in one minute. Points will be given for both form and height on the wall."

We watched Tony, Jason, and Dennis as they skated toward the parallel banks set up in the center of the skatepark. Three members of the El Tigre team were already there. They looked good as they warmed up, but I was sure our guys were better.

In the bank riding event, the members of both teams speed down one bank, then climb another with the momentum of their run, kick turning when they'd reached the highest point they could without slipping back down, then riding down and up the other bank again.

The event was like bank riding, with the members of both teams speeding down the ramp, then climbing another with the momentum of their run, kick turning when they'd reached the highest point they could without slipping back down, then riding the board down and up the other ramp again.

Jason was doing great, and from where I sat it looked as though Dennis and Tony were sure going higher than the members of the other team, but we had to wait to hear the judges' decision. It only took a couple of minutes.

"According to the judges," the announcer said, "the L.A. Wheels have the edge on this event."

Next was the freestyle, and the girls went out for that one. The El Tigres didn't have a chance. We won just about all the freestyle points.

All excited, Millicent hugged both Jenny and Randi when the announcer gave the news. "This is my first time ever to see real skateboarding," she said. "It's fantastic. I wouldn't have believed how exciting it can be!"

"Especially when you're part of the team, it is," Randi said.

I watched Manny, sitting on one of the benches next to Dennis, making sure he got his wheels tightened up right. Dennis probably knew how to do it a lot better than Manny did, but I think Manny felt he had to supervise everything we did. He was beginning to really push us to practice these days, and while he seemed pretty happy when we won the first two events of the night, he couldn't seem to relax. Maybe he would if we came out ahead at the end of the competition. Maybe he thought it was too soon to tell. I thought he'd changed lately. When we first met him he was eager and optimistic, but he seemed to get more uptight as we skated more, acting as though his life depended on us being tops at everything.

The high jump event was coming up, and Peter was going out for that. I didn't hear just how high the bar was the last time Peter cleared it, but his El Tigre opponent didn't make it. He knocked the bar down, and Peter won.

The announcer's voice came over the mike. "El Tigre will have a tough time matching the L.A. Wheels' perfect score. Oh, that miss put El Tigre ten points behind, according to the final readout."

Tony, Jason, and I were in the relay race. That was the only event Manny would let me enter tonight, because of the shoulder, even though it was better now. He told me to take it easy for a while, until I was sure there'd be no trouble.

We started off into the snake course, racing around the zigzag banked 1000' concrete switchback course, handing a little flag to the next team member waiting to race.

Tony and the El Tigre who started first were even until the last switchback, when Tony streaked ahead. He was still ahead when he shoved the flag into my hand, and I held my own with the El Tigre who raced with me. It was great to be skating again! I was ahead of the El Tigre when I got the flag to Jason and moved quickly to the sidelines to cheer him on.

Somehow he lost ground and the El Tigre surged ahead of him until they got to the last turn, when Jason put on a spurt of speed you wouldn't believe, and raced across the fnish line. The crowd roared, and our team went crazy. The announcer was the only one in the place who kept his cool.

"You've just seen professional skateboarding at its finest, ladies and gentlemen. We'll be having full competition every Friday night, so get your tickets early."

Crowds of people swarmed around us, mostly chicks who headed for Jason, reaching to touch him and trying to talk to him. Manny didn't care much for that. He formed us into a group and managed to get us out the back door. We got on the bus before the crowd found us again, and then they surrounded the bus, tapping on the windows, waving to all of us, blowing kisses to Jason.

I think Randi and Manny were the only two who didn't love all that attention. When some of the chicks smiled and waved at me, I knew how Elton John must feel; but Randi kept watching Jason to see how he was taking it, and looking as though she'd like to kill them all.

Manny was in the driver's seat, with Millicent standing beside him. He tried to get the bus slowly through the people, but it was hard to move without hitting somebody, and they didn't seem to want to get out of the way.

"Can you believe these kids?" he shouted. "What are they trying to do?"

"Oh, come on, Manny," Millicent said. "These are the kids who'll be your biggest audiences. They'll bring their friends next time, just to see the L.A. Wheels."

"Yeah?" Manny didn't sound too convinced. "Well, right now they're a nuisance." He opened the door a crack so he could call to them. "Come on, get away. Let me drive out of here! Please!"

Millicent kept trying to soothe him. "This is what it's like when you're famous, Manny. Hey, you're on your way!"

The motel we stopped in that night was a little better than we'd been getting. Maybe it was because of the big win we'd had that evening, or maybe Manny was trying to impress Millicent. The room I was sharing with Dennis and Peter had carpeting on the floor and some easy chairs, as well as the beds and the table. We were sitting around reading magazines and going over the big victory over the El Tigres when Tony came in.

"What happened, Tony?" I asked him. "You get

kicked out of your room again?"

He gave me a disgusted look. "Yeah. I'm just a third bird in their little love nest." He sat down and grabbed the magazine out of my hands.

"Hey! I was reading that!" I tried to grab it back.

Tony swung it above his head so I couldn't get it without knocking him down. "I haven't seen it yet. It's the new *Skateboard,* isn't it?"

"Yeah, big star," I said. "And I paid for it."

He began leafing through it. "That's okay, big star. I bought the last one and let you read it."

"Are you both big stars?" Dennis asked. He was on the floor beside Peter, who was teaching him how to play blackjack.

"Sure. We all are," I said. "You are too. Didn't you see how the chicks worship us? First thing you know, we'll be bigger than Donnie and Marie. We'll have chicks throwing themselves under our skateboards, begging us to skate on them. We'll have mansions in Beverly Hills, and drive Ferraris."

"I can't drive a Ferrari. I'm not old enough to get a driver's license."

"You can hire a chauffeur," Peter told him. "Do you want me to hit those two kings, or not?"

"No way," Dennis said. "And my twenty beats your eighteen. Pay up."

"You sure you've never played blackjack before?" Peter squinted at Dennis suspiciously.

"No, but I get A's in arithmetic." Dennis grabbed the candy bar lying beside Peter, and put it with the one he'd bet.

Tony held up the magazine, showing us a picture of a bowl-shaped reservoir. "Here's the 'toilet bowl.' You guys ever skate in it?"

"No," Peter said. "By the time I found out it was in Los Angeles, they'd trashed the place."

"I rode it," Dennis said.

"Sure you did!" Tony frowned at him.

"I did so! Two years ago, when I was eight. Just before they put in the speed bumps. You never believe anything I say."

"Why should I?"

Dennis was whining now. "You never tell me anything either." Sometimes he could be bratty, and this was one of the times.

"Like what?" Tony said.

"Like why did you get kicked out of your room tonight?"

Peter started to laugh. "You're too young, twerp!"

"I'm not too young. It's because Jason and Randi are kissing in there, isn't it?"

"Hey," I said. "You'd better not go saying things like that in front of Manny or Millicent."

Dennis gave me a scornful look. "Hey, what do you think? No way!"

"Then cool it," Peter told him. "Turn over your cards."

"Blackjack!" Dennis said. "Pay up again!"

"Lucky! I'm not playing with you anymore." Peter collected the cards and handed Dennis another candy bar.

Dennis unwrapped it and chewed it thoughtfully. "One thing I can't understand. Why does Jason want to hang around with a girl?"

We all cracked up.

"See, twerp, I told you you were too young," Peter said.

Dennis looked hurt. "She's so stuck up."

"Who? Randi?" Tony asked. "She's got a lot more to be stuck up about than you do."

I agreed with him. Randi was something special. It was too bad she never looked at anybody except Jason. She never seemed to notice me, and I didn't have any chance in the world of getting her away from him.

But I had daydreams sometimes that I was a hot skater like Jason. I could even dream that he dropped out of the team and left Randi, and she went for me then. You can tell they were daydreams, all right, because if Jason ever quit the team I'd be the last one to be able to take his place. With everybody counting on me to win like they did on Jason, I'd go to pieces.

I knew that because it happened once. I let everybody down that time, and I always remember how awful it felt. It was a few years back, when I was in Little League baseball. My dad was really gung-ho on Little League, and to please him, I used to practice every spare minute until I'd worked my way up to be the team's best pitcher. Then, the last game of the season, in the last inning, when the score was tied, the coach told me to go in there and win. My folks were cheering in the bleachers so loud that they sounded like a whole ball park full of people.

And I got so nervous with everyone counting on me, I just couldn't throw my curve ball. The other team's batter made a home run.

It wasn't that anyone blamed me for losing the game. The coach told me it was just bad luck, and my dad told me I'd given it a good try. The guys on the team didn't say much because we all felt rotten, but I knew what everyone was thinking. They'd counted on me to win, and I'd gone to pieces.

That's why I could only daydream . . . about being a hot skater, and about being as good as Jason . . . and about Randi.

Tony was pacing restlessly. "If we had some wheels, we could split somewhere."

Peter nodded. "Yeah, but there's nothing around here that's within walking distance."

I didn't say anything. I only had a dollar sixty in my pocket and that wouldn't buy much, even if we had wheels. I wished Manny would come up with some pay.

Chapter 12

Manny lay back against the pillows of the bed, leafing through a magazine. The walls of the motel rooms must be thin, because he could hear someone strumming a guitar. Sounded pretty good. It must be Millicent. Her room was next to his.

He laid the magazine on his stomach and just listened to the music for a while, letting his thoughts drift. Was Randi in her own room tonight? He'd check later and see. If she wasn't, he'd ask Millicent to talk to her tomorrow. It was good to have a woman handling that kind of stuff. The kids seemed to like her a lot.

His eyes were closing, so he reached over to switch off the light, and then he lay in the darkness, half-awake, the music lulling him. He could hear the cars that passed on the highway, and the sounds of laughter from one of the other rooms. Probably Peter and Brad. Sounded like them. Somewhere in the distance an animal was howling, and nearby there was the sound of scraping metal.

Scraping metal! The sound was right here in this

room! Manny sat up and saw the door swinging open and the light from the corridor shining in.

"What's going on?" Manny said.

A dark form was coming through the door, closing it behind him. Then an explosion of light hit Manny's face. He blinked into the flashlight's beam. "Who is it? What do you want?"

The man approached the bed silently, waving a cigarette whose glowing tip made red arcs of fire in the darkness outside the flashlight beam. "Hello, Manny. Sol sent me. He wants his money."

"What's with him? I told him the end of the month." Manny could hear the fear in his own voice that tightened it and made it quiver. Sol's friends didn't make night visits just to say hello.

"Sol said that wasn't good enough," the dark shape said, and the flashlight beam went out.

Manny's voice rose to a frightened squeal. "What are you going to do?"

"Let's just call this the appetizer. Let's hope I don't have to serve the main course."

The shape in the darkness moved towards the bed.

Millicent was trying hard to get the chords right. It was the C-minor seventh that was giving her trouble. She tried again, but was suddenly aware of noises in the room next to hers. That was Manny's room. That was his voice that became a sudden yelp of terror! Now something banged against the wall, making a horrible thud.

Millicent jumped off the bed and ran to put her ear against the wall. Whatever was going on in there didn't sound good, but she wasn't sure of what to do. Scream? Call the police? Well, she couldn't just stand here!

Then, suddenly, the noises stopped and she heard a door bang shut. She opened her own door and stepped out into the corridor, hearing the motor of a car outside roaring. She stood still, listening to it fade into the distance.

Breathless, frightened, she knocked on Manny's door. There was no answer. She opened it cautiously, and spoke to the dark shape that lay on the bed. "Manny? Are you all right?"

His answer was a groan.

She moved anxiously to the bed and switched on the bedside lamp. Manny lay there, shaking, his eyes closed, his face red and beginning to swell. She touched it gently. "Here, let me see."

Manny jerked away from her. He seemed embarrassed. "It's nothing," he said. "I'm fine. Really."

"I'm a nurse, remember?" She examined the cuts on his eye and cheek, then got a washcloth from the bathroom, wet it, and brought it back. She dabbed his face as carefully as she could. "Your friends play rough."

"You heard?"

"The walls aren't exactly soundproof."

"You think the kids. . . ?"

"Mine is the only room near yours. Of course, I don't know how you'll explain that shiner to them."

"What shiner?" Manny's fingers went up to touch his swelling eye.

"The one you're going to have in the morning," Millicent said. "I'm going to my room to get some stuff to dress the cuts. I'll only be a minute."

She went back to her room and picked up her kit. Then she saw the bottle of vodka she kept with her things, and picked that up, too. A stiff drink might help Manny. She felt sick about what whoever-it-was had done to him. He was in bad trouble, but he'd kept it pretty well hidden until now. She wished he trusted her enough to tell her about it. Maybe two of them could figure out something that could be done about it; but then she knew him well enough by now to know he didn't usually complain.

She went back to his room, spread her medical supplies out on the bed, and began to dab iodine on his wounds. "You want a drink?"

Manny still seemed to be dazed. "Huh?"

"A drink. I brought over some vodka. I think you could use one, and I could too. What have you got for mixer?"

Manny glanced at the styrofoam cooler standing in the corner of the room. "There's some Mountain Dew left."

"You call that a mixer?" She put gauze over the cuts, and fixed it with adhesive tape. Then she got two glasses from the bathroom, went to the cooler, and put some of the ice cubes in both glasses. She picked up a can of Mountain Dew and took it back to Manny's bed. "I'm having my vodka straight," she said. "Do you want this stuff with it?"

He nodded weakly. Millicent made the drinks, handed one to him, and sat on the edge of the bed. "You owe them much?"

"Who?" he asked.

"The strong-arm boys. *Them.*"

"Enough."

"Can you get it?" she asked softly.

He shrugged, then winced at the pain it caused. "Who knows?" Then he propped himself gingerly on one elbow and sipped at his drink. "Who knows?" he repeated, but Millicent, watching him, thought *he* knew very well. He knew that unless the L.A. Wheels started drawing big crowds and making some money, Manny Bloom was going to suffer for it. A lot.

Chapter 13

In a secluded corner of an empty parking lot, Jason was doing wheelies. It was another practice session at the park, and the L.A. Wheels were working hard to get in the best shape possible for the Palmdale competition, but Jason found that he was practicing more and enjoying it less. All of a sudden it had turned into hard, grinding work, not the fun thing it used to be. They'd been here all morning, and he was tired of jumping and racing. He was tired of Manny on his back all the time, pushing him to do more. That's why he'd found this quiet place to be by himself.

But he wasn't alone for long. Tony was skating up to him, calling. "Hey, Jason! Manny wants you to come back and practice with the rest of us."

"Okay," Jason said, but he kept on with the wheelies.

Tony sounded breathless. "He's got everyone looking all over for you, man!"

"Let them look," Jason said. "I'll be there in a minute."

Then he saw Manny, jogging up the path toward them, red-faced and out of breath, his swollen eye glinting purple in the sunlight.

"What are you doing here, Jason?"

"Nothing."

Manny was pretty mad. "Will you stop messing around and get back to practice? Palmdale's in two weeks!"

"Okay, okay," Jason said.

"It's not okay! We've got another team to beat, remember?"

"Yeah. I remember."

Manny put his fists on his hips. "I don't think you *do* remember. Not by your lazy attitude these last few days."

Jason was getting angry, but he wasn't going to show it. He just shrugged and pushed his skateboard back and forth with one foot. "Get off my case, will you?"

"I'll get off your case when you start moving!" Manny turned away and started down the path again, but Jason could hear the word he muttered as he went. "Star!"

They watched him go around the bend in the path, then Tony whistled. "What's with him?"

"Who knows? He's been burnt out ever since he got that shiner."

"Ever since he hired that nurse, man! That's when it started." Tony popped a bubble. "Maybe he's got the hots for her."

"She can do better than him. A *lot* better." Jason got on his board and began rolling slowly back to the practice area, Tony following.

But in the days that followed, Jason felt that

Manny was picking on him. He had to make every move perfectly, or practice it until he could. The hours were long and the rest periods were few, and it was okay for Manny to say they weren't working hard enough. He just sat around watching the practice, drinking his Mountain Dew. But Jason went along with it. He wanted the team to win at Palmdale, too.

Finally the team was on the bus, driving along the desert highway toward Palmdale, the sun hot on the sand around them, the bus tires grinding up clouds of dust as they turned into a lonely gas station-general store in the middle of nowhere.

An elderly man in jeans, his face wrinkled from years of squinting in the desert sunlight, approached the bus.

Manny poked his head out the window. "Five bucks of regular."

The attendant looked surprised, Jason noted. Probably figured the bus should take ethyl.

Manny looked at the price on the pumps. "Seventy-five cents! Wow!" He turned around to talk to the team. "I'm going into the store for a candy bar. Anybody want anything?"

"How about some potato chips?" Brad called.

"Yeah," Jason said, "and a cold drink. It's hot. How about a six-pack of cold Schlitz?"

Manny acted as though he hadn't heard, and Jason knew the remark about beer hadn't made him happy. Manny had it all worked out what the team members should eat and drink while they were training.

Beside him, Randi said, "Maybe we should cool the bad vibes for a while, Jason."

"Bad vibes?" Jason was surprised. Randi could

see what was going on. She wasn't stupid. "Maybe you haven't noticed, but he's been on my case pretty regular."

"Maybe *you* haven't noticed," Randi said, "but he's been on mine, too."

"Since when have you been such a pal of his?" Jason felt hurt.

"It's not that," Randi said softly. "Oh, I know I didn't like him much at first. But now I can see he counts on you, just like we all do. He wants you to be better than just good. And he wants the team to be great."

"Well he sure has a weird way of going about it," Jason said. "I know one thing. I don't like the pressure he's putting on. If he doesn't let up, he's going to have one less skater on the team."

"You wouldn't quit, would you?" Randi stared at him. "We wouldn't have a team, then. All the other guys would leave, if you did."

Jason folded his arms. "I don't know. I just know I want him off my act, that's all." He looked out the window and saw Manny coming out of the store, carrying a big bag of potato chips in one hand and a six-pack of beer in the other. He climbed on the bus and threw the beer toward Jason. "Here. This is for *after* the meet."

He started the bus and drove on.

Jason caught the beer, feeling stupid. Manny wasn't a bad dude; he knew that. He really liked him pretty well. It was just that he didn't like being ordered around, pushed into things. He'd had a lot of that from his dad and from the teachers in school. There was always so much to do, so much that had to be done—chores around the house, and homework, and exams to get ready for, and classes to attend. Jason knew he wasn't lazy; it was just that he liked to do things his own way. He knew he could get things done and do them well, but he liked to do them in his own time . . . the way he wanted. That's why he enjoyed surfing so much, and why he liked skateboarding. He could be out there by himself, doing his own thing, knowing he was good and knowing it was only him doing it. He didn't do it because he was told to, or because somebody expected him to, or because he *had* to. It was something that was all his.

He was pretty sure Manny didn't understand that.

Brad Harris (Leif Garrett) at skatepark

Filming of downhill
invitational at Burbank

Leif Garrett and Ellen Oneal
two skate wheelie

Jason (Rich Van Der Wyk) backside kickturn

Peter (Steve Monahan) at 1st LA Wheels exhibition

Peter (Steve Monahan) jumps over Manny's car

Jenny (Ellen Oneal) 'two board daffy' on skateboards

Tony Bluetile (Tony Alva) practicing slalom

Little Dennis (David Hyde) at team practice

Manny, Nurse Millicent (Kathleen Lloyd) and
Randi celebrate at Palmdale

Jason (Rich Van Der Wyk) and Randi (Pam Kenneally)
discuss Manny on Malibu beach

Sol (Anthony Carbone),
Manny's reluctant backer
threatens Manny over the
phone

Brad (Leif Garrett) after his
big victory at Burbank

Team pose in front of LA Wheels bus

Tony Bluetile (Tony Alva)
coaches Brad (Leif Garrett)
for downhill race

Tony Bluetile (Tony Alva), Brad (Leif Garrett) and Jenny (Ellen Oneal) in Manny's car driving to find other team members.

Jenny (Ellen Oneal) and Brad (Leif Garrett) at the pool; their first day with Manny

Manny (Allen Garfield) and Millicent (Kathleen Lloyd)
at bar after 1st victory

Brad (Leif) with Craig Chaquico of the Jefferson Starship before their big race

Brad (Leif) with Gaffer and camera on the set

Manny before meeting Millicent at restaurant

Young Dennis (David Hyde)
with team

Chapter 14

The Palmdale auditorium was nearly full, Manny noted. Maybe at last the word was spreading, and more people were finding out that skateboarding was exciting to watch. For the first time in many weeks, he felt really great. His team was in top shape, and the crowd was enthusiastic. There were only two problems that bothered him.

Jason was one problem. What was bugging him? The other problem was whether or not the Wheels could win the competition tonight. If his star skater didn't perform well, the team would lose. If his team lost to the Malibu Coasters tonight, Sol would hear about it. If Sol heard about it, he'd be even more worried about his investment; and if he worried, that was bad for Manny.

He sat down on the end of one of the benches, where the kids were busy tightening the trucks of their skateboards and checking their wheels. Millicent, beside him, reached into the cooler for a Mountain Dew.

"Here, Manny. Drink this and relax!"

He grinned at her. "Hey, I feel great. How about you?"

"Sure. We're going to win, I can feel it."

The first event was the high jump. Peter and Tony went out to warm up on the floor, while the others called encouragement to them from the sidelines.

The two skaters from the Malibu Coasters team were ready to make their jump. Two poles had been set up with a bar between the cross bar set at three-foot-six. The audience watched, quieting as they approached the bar together, wheels purring.

Manny admired their good coordination as they cleared the bar together, but only one of them landed on his skateboard after the jump. The shorter of the two missed his entirely. He'd sent it under the bar too fast.

"That's a big miss for the Malibu Coasters at three-foot-six in the high jump," the announcer said. "There's a good chance for the L.A. Wheels to pick up three points now."

Peter and Tony skated out to the center of the auditorium.

"Tony Bluetile," the announcer said, "and Peter 'the Wolf' Steffens from the L.A. Wheels, who will attempt to go the three-foot-six height. Here they come."

Manny tensed as they skated towards the bar. They looked good. All the practicing was paying off. They jumped in perfect unison, cleared the bar with inches to spare, and landed on their boards at the same time. Manny cheered. They were great!

The crowd gave them a lot of applause as the announcer's voice rose above the noise. "A magnificent jump, ladies and gentlemen! A beautiful jump! Another three points for the L.A. Wheels. And now we'll move right on to the freestyle event."

Jenny, Randi, and Dennis were already out on the floor: Jenny doing her best handstand; Dennis in a shoot-the-duck crouched position with his leg held forward and his arms stretched parallel to the board; Randi whirling in a series of three-sixties.

The Malibu Coasters had their best freestyle skaters out, too, and they were doing well. They had Laura Thornhill and Ed Nadalin, two of the best freestylers anywhere. Manny listened to the announcer, trying to gauge which skaters were making the biggest impression.

"Look at that jump and the handstand from Ed Nadalin of the Coasters! Beautiful, kid! Aren't they amazing, folks? He was barefoot, too!"

There were scattered bursts of cheers and applause. Manny could see the rest of the team members watching anxiously, too. They had to keep those points they'd gained!

"There's Jenny Bradshaw using two boards at one time, doing the daffy, ladies and gentlemen. One per foot for Jenny! And look at Laura Thornhill and Bob Biniak doing those spinners!"

Manny had to admit the Coasters contestants were good. They were giving a flashy performance jumping off their moving skateboards, hands high in the air, spinning completely around and landing perfectly on their boards again.

The whistle blew and the announcer spoke again. "That ends the freestyle, ladies and gentlemen. Let's have a big round of applause. They're all fine skaters. And it looks like . . . a three-point lead for the Malibu Coasters, coming out of the freestyle. Keeping it close; keeping it very, very tight competition."

Jenny, Dennis, and Randi came back to the bench, looking unhappy. Manny went over to talk to them.

"Hey, you were all great! Don't let it get you. We win a little . . . we lose a little."

"Yeah, but three whole points!" Jenny made a sour face.

"Those guys are really good!" Dennis said.

Manny nodded. "Yeah, they are. Good competition. We'll have to practice some more of that stuff the Coasters were laying on them out there."

"Yeah," Dennis said. "Wait until next time, you guys!"

Now barrels were being set up in a row in the center of the auditorium, and Tony was skating out there with the member of the Coasters team who'd be jumping against him.

Tony would be okay, Manny thought. He was hard to beat. It was Jason who worried him most. He glanced at Jason, sitting next to Brad, waiting for their turn. Manny wished he knew what was eating Jason. He could understand Brad better—a good, steady skater with beautiful balance but no self-confidence. Brad and the others thought Jason was the whole team, and Manny supposed they were right, in a way. It was for sure if Jason wasn't on the team, they wouldn't have so much going for them.

The announcer's voice interrupted his thoughts. "Going into the barrel jump now, Tony Bluetile once again representing the Los Angeles team and

competing against a young man we haven't met yet
tonight, Hubie Kerns for the Malibu Coasters.
Hubie is coming up now, getting ready to jump . . .
forward and over!"

The Malibu skater landed short and fell. The
crowd gave out a shocked cry, but relaxed as they
saw him get up smiling and brush himself off. He'd
rolled as he fell, to break the impact, and was unin-
jured.

"The young man is all right, ladies and gentlemen," the announcer assured them. "Now Tony
is going to take off. He's going to jump sixteen barrels. And there he goes!"

Tony leaped the barrels easily, clearing them,
landing on the skateboard that waited at the end of
the line, and finishing with a smooth glide.

The whole team was jumping up and down,
cheering. Manny turned to see Millicent beside
him, her eyes shining. "Great!" she said. "Even if
we lose the rest, we could still win. Right!"

"I think so. Yeah."

Jenny had heard what she said. "We're not losing any more points, Millie! No way!"

Millicent smiled at her. "All right!"

Jason and Brad were leaving the bench while the
announcer told the audience about the next event.
"In this fascinating, action-packed, ramp riding
event, the judges are giving points for grace, speed,
height, and form. A fall can be very costly. This is
the first time these new, fifteen-foot-high ramps
have been used in sanctioned competition. The
skaters will ride down one ramp and up the other,
kick turn at the top, and back down and up the
first ramp."

There were shouts of "Come on Jason!" and

"Ride with it, Brad!" from the L.A. Wheels watching the event, and Manny found himself muttering under his breath, tensing as though he were climbing the ramps himself. "Come on, guys, get up there! Make it good!"

They did make it good. Both boys went higher and moved more fluidly than either of their Malibu Coaster opponents. It was obvious who was going to win, but the announcer made it official.

"And there is another three points for the Los Angeles Wheels."

Millicent hugged Manny, Jenny and Dennis grinned at each other, and the other kids cheered.

"We're moving now into the slalom competition," the announcer said. "Slalom, as you are aware, is similar to skiing and ice skating, the same kind of competition. We will have three divisions, the first ones doubling right back. This event features the man who does everything for the L.A. Wheels, Tony Bluetile, and his competition from the Malibu Coasters, Bobby Piercy! Are you ready, gentlemen?"

Tony and Bobby stood at the top of the ramp. Red rubber cones had been set about six feet apart in a slalom pattern. At the sound of the whistle they both took off, skating between the cones, swerving in a narrow, spiraling course.

Maybe Tony was tiring, Manny thought. The Coaster contestant was pulling ahead of him, finishing first. "Okay, Brad," he shouted. "Get in there and win!"

"The second heat," the announcer said, "will be Brad Harris for the L.A. Wheels and Rene Carrasco for Malibu. All right, gentlemen, stand by."

Whistles and cheers sounded as the skaters

rushed down the ramp, weaving between the cones.

"Brad Harris is looking good," said the announcer. "Brad has got Carrasco . . . and he wins!"

"One more win," Manny thought, pacing nervously. "Come on, Jason, give us one more win."

Millicent was cheering beside him, and Jenny and the others were stamping their feet, shouting Jason on.

The loudspeaker boomed out its message. "Jason Maddox will now face Malibu's star performer, Chad McQueen. And they're off!"

Jason started slowly, so that the Coaster was a cone ahead of him most of the way down. Manny held his breath until Jason had caught up with and passed him.

"It's Maddox by inches!" the announcer cheered.

"We've won!" Millicent gave Manny a wild hug. "Let me take you out for a victory drink afterwards, after we drop off the kids. Okay?"

Manny felt limp and happy. "You can take me out for as many drinks as you like!"

Manny drove the now-empty bus, and Millicent followed him in her Porsche, to a very western-looking bar with decor that reminded Manny of an old John Wayne movie, all flocked wallpaper and crystal chandeliers. At one end of the room, a small group played country-western music and a man in cowboy boots and hat sang loudly.

They sat at a small table in a darkened corner, both of them tired and happy after winning the meet, and they talked about how elated the kids had been, and how the crowds at the auditorium had enjoyed the performance.

"Didn't it feel good?" Millicent said. "It seems to be all coming together."

"Yeah," Manny agreed. "I've got to say it felt good. We've been waiting long enough."

A waitress came to take their order, and Manny asked for a pitcher of beer. When she left he continued speaking his thoughts out loud. "It's taken time to develop, but I think we're on the right track now. We almost had a full house tonight!" The memory was so good he laughed out loud. "Can you believe it? A full house in the middle of the desert!"

The waitress returned with the pitcher of beer. Manny poured a glass for Millicent and a little for himself. "You know what I've been wanting to ask you?"

"What?"

"Why did you ever take this crazy job?"

She pulled a cigarette from the package she'd put on the table, and Manny lit it for her. She looked at him through the smoke. "Maybe I needed the money. Not that I've seen that much of it."

Manny felt a little embarrassed. He'd explained to her about that—how the team wasn't breaking even yet, and when the money started coming in, she'd be paid. "With more crowds like tonight's, it shouldn't be long now," he said. "But you could make better money somewhere else."

"You trying to get rid of me?" she grinned.

"No way! But I just wondered. . . ."

"Well, Bloom, I don't know about you, but my parents were the type that drummed it into my head that I had to prepare for a career . . . to fall back on, just in case."

"In case what?"

Her laugh was soft and melodious. "In case I didn't get married, I guess."

"And did you?"

"Did I what? Get married?" She suddenly became serious. "No. Did you?"

Manny shuddered at the memory. "Yeah, once. It didn't work out." He took a sip of the beer and poured a fresh glass for her. "You'll be paid, you know."

"Hey, it's okay. Don't worry about it. I know I will." She reached over the table and patted his hand. "I've got enough saved up to live on until we start making money. My Porsche was a present from my folks, and it's paid for. I can wait, so don't worry!" She smiled at him. "This is a great job . . . the best I've ever had. I like all the kids—Jenny, so sweet and talented; Dennis, so smart for his age; and I get a kick out of Tony and Peter, with their joking around. I like Brad too. He seems quieter than the rest of them, and more serious, and a bit shy. And I'd like to get closer to Randi." She took another sip of her beer.

"You haven't mentioned Jason."

"I feel the way the other kids do about Jason. He's terrific."

"Yeah? Well, everyone likes you," Manny said truthfully. "It's really working out. They're really crazy about you."

"Well, they like you, too."

"Oh yeah. They really love me. Especially Jason." Manny shook his head.

"Maybe you're pushing him a little too hard, Manny."

So she'd noticed it too, how Jason was getting

reluctant to practice and seemed to be always turning Manny off. "Honey," he explained, "I've got to push him. He's the best skater we've got. I've got to stay right on him or he'll slack off."

"He's pretty sensitive, though. After all, he's only eighteen, and part of him is boy, and part man. You've got to be careful of that."

She had a point there, Manny thought. "But I can't treat him like a baby," he said.

The singer and the band were finishing up, getting ready to leave.

Millicent leaned forward. "Tonight must have helped you, right?"

"With what? What do you mean?"

"With your money problems."

Manny gave her a wry smile. "Yeah. It helped about as much as putting a band-aid on a leper."

"Really?" She looked unhappy.

Manny nodded. "Don't worry about it," he told her.

Chapter 15

Success was coming at last to the L.A. Wheels. After Palmdale, Manny took his team to San Diego, Santa Barbara, Sacramento, Chico, and points between, and everywhere the crowds became bigger and bigger. Manny hoped the money would get bigger too. He still had to pay off Sol, and every night he went to bed behind bolted doors and locked windows. But he'd be in the clear soon if things kept on this way.

The team was mobbed by autograph hunters and fans. Jason, especially, was the teen-agers' hero. After the team was interviewed by some local TV stations, the mobs of fans got bigger, and every time the Wheels performed, they could count on waiting an hour after the show was over until Jason could get away from his admirers. Manny noticed Randi getting more and more unhappy as the girls squealed over Jason.

Between shows, Manny kept them practicing hard. Now that they were on top, they had to stay there.

He worried about the bus, though. It was too shabby for a team of celebrities to be driving in. He thought he could spare enough to get a good paint job on it so they wouldn't be ashamed to ride in it. Manny could count it as an advertising expense. He supervised the painter, who took a couple of days to do the job, then drove the bus to the skateboard park where the team was supposed to meet that day.

They were practicing. Jenny was doing a handstand with one skateboard on top of another. Brad was walking the dog, and Tony and Peter were chasing each other in a game of skateboard tag. Randi and Dennis were practicing three-sixties. They all stopped and stared at the bus as Manny pulled it into the parking lot, excited to present his team with a "gift." Manny enjoyed the surprised look on their faces.

He'd had a very special paint job done. There was a portrait of Jason, larger than life, painted on the side, and around him were all the team members on their boards, doing their various specialties.

"Far out!" Jenny found her own caricature, and giggled at it.

Tony inspected his. "Hey, that's really primo, man."

"It makes you look almost handsome, Ugly," Brad told him. "But where am I?"

"On the back," Peter pointed out. "Right over the exhaust. I guess that tells us where you belong."

Randi sighed. "I wish you'd put me next to Jason, Manny."

He shrugged. "I didn't want to get the personalities mixed up with the players."

"What are you complaining about?" Jenny said to Randi. "I'm next to Manny."

"Listen, you could have done worse," Manny said. Then he noticed that someone was missing. "Where's Jason?"

Everyone looked embarrassed, but nobody said anything.

"Is everybody deaf?" Manny shouted. "Where is he?" He turned to Randi. "Well?"

Brad and Tony looked very busy inspecting their boards. Peter and Jenny got on theirs and began doing wheelies. Dennis darted behind Randi.

Manny was angry. Jason was supposed to be here, practicing like everybody else. That kid was getting a star complex. "Was he here at all?" he asked, but nobody answered. "Come on, I'm serious. Did he show or not?" Their silence was infuriating. "I'm running a business here. We're on our way, and you're all too dumb to realize it. We got a chance to be part of a gig so big it's going to put skateboarding on the map."

He turned at the sound of a motor. Jason's brother's van pulled into the parking lot, and Jason got out.

Manny was seething. Who did he think he was, looking so calm and unconcerned? "It's about time you got here," he shouted. "You were supposed to be here an hour ago. We've got a chance to enter a national event with teams from all over the country, and you can't even show up for practice."

Jason looked at him coldly, silently, and Randi ran up and put her arms around him.

"Okay," Manny said. "You all told me you

were interested. We're either in it or not. No more hacking around. Can't you kids see what I'm doing for you?" He looked at all the impassive faces watching him and threw up his hands in a gesture of despair. "I don't know why I bother."

Jason stood very still, just looking at him, and tension crackled in the air between them. Manny waited for some kind of excuse, some kind of answer, but there was nothing but that cold silence that was growing unbearable. "Well?" he said, finally.

Jason's voice was low. "What's this big event?"

"The first annual Burbank Downhill Invitational. A one-mile race with twenty thousand dollars first prize! I told you guys I'd make you big time."

"Twenty grand!" Tony threw his skateboard in the air with a whoop.

"Yeah," Manny said. "Twenty thousand. Any of you interested in it? Are you, Jason?"

"Sure," Jason said quietly.

"Then why weren't you out here practicing?"

"I ran out of gas," Jason mumbled.

Manny gave him a scathing look. "This is really something! I'm giving you kids a chance to be pros, so you'd better start acting like pros. That means a professional attitude . . . and that takes practice and discipline."

Jason frowned. "Come on, man! Give us a break!"

"That's right," Manny said forcefully. "Discipline. No breaking training. Lots of hard work. Eight hours' sleep. You catching my drift, hot shot?"

Jason nodded silently, and Manny relaxed. It

was okay. The kids wanted to win, they just didn't realize how much work was involved. And Manny was there to handle that end of it.

He grabbed Jason in a bear hug. "Okay, come on and see your picture. You haven't seen it yet."

Chapter 16

On Sunday we had the day off, and Jenny invited us all over to her house for a swim and barbeque. It was good just to lie in the sun, doing nothing. We'd been practicing pretty hard, and we all needed some time to relax.

I was lying beside the pool, feeling the sun warming my skin, listening to the shushing sounds the water made and the talking of the other guys as they sunned themselves. Then suddenly something wet and cold grabbed my arm and yanked me into the pool. I sank all the way to the bottom, water in my nose and mouth, and when I finally got back to the surface I could see Tony, a few feet away from me, laughing like a hyena.

I chased him around the pool, caught him at the shallow end, and got him in an arm lock, but Jenny broke it up.

"Hey, you guys! My mom will be back soon. She doesn't like rough stuff in the pool."

We got out and collapsed in chairs on the deck.

Jenny's six-year-old brother Andrew was on a skateboard, riding it around the patio.

"When do we eat?" Dennis asked Jenny.

"Pretty soon. My mom's gone to get the hamburgers and fixings." Jenny perched on the edge of the pool, next to Peter.

Dennis clutched at his stomach. "Do we have to wait for Jason and the others before we eat?"

"There's nobody else coming," Jenny said. "Jason and Randi went someplace by themselves. Millicent had friends visiting her, and I don't know what Manny's doing."

"Probably sitting at home, figuring out ways to make us work harder," Peter said.

"Yeah, man," Tony said. "That guy's a fiend for watching other people work." He called out to Jenny's brother. "Far out! All right, Andrew, skate out!"

"Hey, Jenny," Peter said. "You know your mom called mine?"

"I know. She's really ticked off at Manny."

"So's mine," I told them. "She doesn't like me getting home so late all the time."

"Yeah," Tony said. "My old man doesn't even dig Manny. He thinks I should quit the team."

"Are you going to?" I asked him.

Tony shrugged. "I don't know. I guess not. He gave me a hundred bucks. At least he didn't rip me off."

"He gave us a hundred bucks each," I said. "I wonder how much he's making on this? He must be doing pretty good."

"All I know is that Manny paid me last, and all he had left was five dollars. I feel sorry for him. I mean, he did make us pros." Jenny pointed at the kitchen. "Dennis, if you're hungry you can go get some cookies out of the fridge, and bring us back some sodas."

I watched Dennis head for the kitchen. "Where else can we make money skating?" I'd been thinking about that for a while. Even if my folks complained about Manny, I thought I understood him. "He's just super gung-ho for the team, that's all. He's trying to be a big-time coach and get us all to shape up so we'll be the best team around."

Peter looked at me as though he hadn't thought of that before. "Yeah? Well, I'll skate for the dude. I like him, but I just wish he'd lay off Jason's case."

"Yeah," Tony added. "Ever since he got that shiner, it seems that somebody's giving him pressure or something."

Peter laughed. "Yeah, intense pressure. Right on the eye. That's pretty gnarly, too."

Dennis came back with a handful of cookies and his arms full of cans. We all helped ourselves as he came around to each of us, then went over to Andrew.

"Here," he said, holding out a cookie. "You can have this if you'll give me a turn on the board."

"No way!" Andrew skated off. Dennis bit into the cookie and leaned against the picnic table.

"Give Dennis a turn, Andrew!" Jenny said.

"No way!" Andrew tried a three-sixty and the board scooted out from under his feet. He reached down and grabbed it.

"Dennis is our guest," Jenny told him. "You remember what Mom says."

Andrew looked as though he'd like to cry. His face screwed up into the beginnings of a howl; then, as he watched Jenny starting to get up, he reluctantly held the skateboard out to Dennis, who took it happily.

"There's cookies in the kitchen," Dennis told him, and went into a series of perfect three-sixties.

Jenny sat down again. "Let's face it, you guys. Sometimes Jason just doesn't try at practice."

"We all know that some days he's a total space case," I said.

Tony popped the top of his soda can. "Yeah, but some days he really flows, you know. If Manny keeps pushing him, he's going to split."

Jenny leaned back on her elbows and dangled her feet in the water. "If Jason goes, Randi would probably go too. What about the rest of you?"

I thought that one over. What would I do if Jason quit the team? Would the team be any good without him?

Everyone else seemed to be considering it, too. Finally Tony spoke.

"Let's hope Manny lets up. We ain't got a team without Jason."

"We don't have a team without Manny either," I pointed out.

I wondered what I'd do with the rest of the summer if the Los Angeles Wheels dissolved. It was exciting, playing for audiences, competing against other skateboarders. Sure, there was hard work involved, but that was fun too. After all, I'd spent a lot of time on my skateboard before the Wheels had been formed. But maybe it wouldn't be too great if we were losing competitions instead of winning them, and if Jason quit, what chance did we have to win?

Dennis let out a sudden shout. "Here comes your mother, Jenny! Let's eat!"

Chapter 17

It was hard work, practicing for the Downhill Invitational. The kids met first thing in the morning and sometimes went on until after dark, building up their speed, perfecting their techniques, zipping through cones like those that would be used in the slalom races, becoming so familiar with their skateboards that they could make them do anything they wanted. Manny was glad the parents hadn't objected too much to all the time their kids would be spending away from home. They seemed to know that this was the big one, the most important meet the L.A. Wheels had had yet, and it was vital that they win.

He was leaning against the bus, munching on a drumstick from the bucket of chicken he'd bought for their lunch. They were parked in Will Rogers State Park, on a hill that wound downward in a steep slope he figured might approximate the slope at Stough Park, where the Burbank Invitational was to be held. The boys were doing a slalom, and the girls were resting inside the bus, Millicent with them.

As Tony walked past him, Manny shouted at him. "Come on, hurry it up! The more time you spend going up the hill, the less runs you'll get in."

Millicent came out of the bus, a hot container of coffee in one hand and a cheese Danish in the other. "Don't you think you're going a little too heavy on the kids?"

"Don't you think you ought to mind your own business?" he snapped.

Millicent flushed. "It seems to me it *is* my business."

"It seems to me you're forgetting what I hired you for."

She looked angry. "And what was that?"

"To be a nurse. To take care of a kid in case he gets hurt." He turned away from her. "And not to be a psychiatrist."

She grabbed his sleeve and tugged it so that he had to turn around and face her. "Maybe you'd prefer to have me talk to the parents!"

Manny was getting mad. "What do you want from me? I'm in debt up to my eyeballs, guys are tenderizing my face, and I've got a bunch of kids who are too lazy to even practice!"

Her voice grew softer. "Manny, they've been practicing six and seven hours a day."

Her tone was soothing, and her eyes were so gentle and sad-looking that he was sorry he'd yelled at her. "Okay, okay," he said. "I'm feeling a little uptight. Time's running out."

"I know the pressure you're under, but they're only kids."

"Only kids!" He shook his head. "I was out on

my own when I was their age. Working my tail off. They're getting paid for having fun."

Tony was gliding past them, curving through the cones of the slalom course, when his skateboard hit one and he tumbled off. Millicent ran to him.

Manny was going towards them when someone touched his arm. He turned to see a white-haired man in a gray suit standing beside him, a briefcase in his hand.

"Mr. Bloom?"

"That's right," Manny said, wondering who this could be.

"Nice to see you!" The man grabbed his right hand and began pumping it. "My name's Charlie Martin. Great little team you've got here. Great little team!"

Manny looked over to Tony, who was being helped to his feet by Millicent. "You okay?" he called, and Tony nodded.

"Just a few scrapes."

"I'll patch him up," Millicent said.

Manny turned back to Mr. Martin. "What can I do for you?"

"I can do something for you and your team, Mr. Bloom. I represent the Yani Skateboard Equipment Company."

"Never heard of you," Manny said, wishing the man would go away. Time was so short, and he couldn't spare much of it listening to pests.

Martin didn't seem to notice his impatience. He went on talking enthusiastically. "We have a whole new line coming out—skateboards, arm pads, leg pads, knee pads . . ." He reached into his case and pulled out a helmet. "This is the new crash helmet that we have. It looks like a professional one, but it's a little less expensive. You haven't heard of Yani yet because we're not big yet, but we're going to be big. We'd like to take you right along with us."

Manny eyed the helmet without enthusiasm, then noticed Jason walking slowly past them. "Hey," he called. "Just go up the hill, all right? Do you need any help?"

"Relax," Jason said mildly. "It's a beautiful day."

Martin was dangling the helmet in front of Manny's face. "I've talked to the management of our company, and they want to use one of your kids in the television commercial."

Manny felt a sudden spark of interest. "TV?"

"Yeah. Television. Nationwide commercial," Martin said grandly. "We can help each other." He stretched his hands wide apart, the helmet dangling by its strap in one of them, apparently illustrating the limitless vistas stretching ahead of them. "I'll tell you what. Why don't we use Jason Maddox, your star? How's that?"

"In the commercial?"

Martin nodded. "Right. And that's only the beginning. This could be big. Talk shows . . ." he lowered his voice again. "Of course you'd have to accompany Jason. You wouldn't mind that?"

Manny kept his voice cool, but joy bubbled inside him. "No, I wouldn't mind."

"Good! We'd like to shoot the commercial the day after tomorrow. Now, I know this is rather sudden—"

Manny interrupted him. "What do I have to do?"

"Nothing. Just bring your boy here to the park at six thirty."

"Six thirty?" Manny wondered how he'd get Jason out that early.

Martin smiled broadly. "They start early in that business."

While Manny talked with the stranger outside the bus, inside Millicent put gauze on Tony's scrapes. "Okay? Feel better?" she asked him.

"Sure does. I'll get back to practicing before Manny starts spitting nails out there."

At the back of the bus, Randi sat by herself, staring sadly out the window. It worried Millicent to see her look that way. She went down the aisle of the bus and sat beside the girl.

"Why the long face, Randi?"

Randi didn't even glance at her. "I'm just watching the guys practice."

"They can't be that bad!" Millicent pulled a cigarette pack out of her purse and offered one to Randi.

She shook her head. "Those things aren't good for you."

Millicent lit a match and puffed on the cigarette. "I know. But we don't always do the things we know are good for us, do we?"

Randi looked puzzled. "Meaning what?"

"Nothing really," Millicent said. "But sitting here by yourself being sad isn't good. If something's bothering you, spit it out. It might help if you did."

Randi curled her long legs up on the seat beside her. "I was just thinking about Jason, and how all the girls are crazy about him now that he's a big star."

"But Jason still likes you best," Millicent pointed out.

"Sure. We love each other. But maybe someday one of those fans of his will look better to him than I do."

Millicent looked closely at Randi's pretty, heart-shaped face and her deep blue eyes, and saw the fear there. "Maybe one day you'll find someone who looks better to *you* than Jason does," she said softly.

Randi shook her head so hard that her long hair fell across her face. "Oh no! I'll never love anyone else. Jason is my whole world."

Millicent thought for a moment, searching for the right thing to say, but nothing came. She could only tell Randi how she herself felt. "There's no security in anyone else, no matter how much you might love them. There's only security in here"— she pointed her finger at her chest—"in yourself. When you have that you can accept love if it comes to you, and you can accept if it leaves you."

"But how do you get secure in yourself?"

Millicent thought about that one. "I'm not sure. Maybe it comes with time. Maybe you have to work at it. Maybe you just have to know that you're a bright, beautiful person and a good skater, and you've got a wonderful, exciting life ahead of you."

Randy's smile seemed to glow. "You mean *me?*"

"I mean you."

Randi was still smiling when she left the bus, but it wasn't until the girl was gone that Millicent thought about what Manny had said, that he hadn't hired her to be a psychiatrist. Well, she wasn't trying to be a psychiatrist. She was only trying to be a friend to these kids she had grown to like so much. She looked out the window at Manny, red-faced, shouting at Peter as he rode down the slope. It wouldn't hurt Manny to try to be a bit more of a friend to them too, she thought.

Chapter 18

Sunset on the ocean stained the water, making a blood-red path across the dark green. Jason and Randi walked hand in hand along the beach, not talking, listening to the sound of the breaking waves and the squawking of sea birds. When they came to a formation of rocks, Jason sat down, pulled a can of beer from his jacket pocket, opened it, and began to drink from it. Randi settled herself beside him, her head on his shoulder.

"Are you ever going to say anything?" she asked him finally.

"Like what?"

"Like what's bugging you."

He passed her the can of beer to take a sip. "I don't know," he said quietly. "It all used to be so much fun. Somehow now it's become a real bummer." He took the can back from her. "You used to be able to skate anywhere. Reservoirs . . . spillways. It was mellow. Then they started speed bumping everything. You have to look around for weeks to find an empty pool."

"Except now we're too busy practicing to try to find one."

"Yeah. It just used to be different."

Randi sat up and looked at him. "I used to have you all to myself, too. Now I'm beginning to wonder."

He put his arms around her. "Aw . . . those chicks don't get to me, baby. You're the only thing that makes sense." He kissed her, tasting the sea-salt the ocean breeze had left on her mouth.

After a while Randi said, "That isn't all that's bugging you, is it?"

He looked out at the heaving waves. "I guess not."

"Is it Manny?"

"Not Manny exactly. More like one of his friends."

"What friend? You mean that creepy-looking guy who was talking to him today at practice?"

"That's the one." Jason tossed a small pebble into the water.

"What did he want?"

"Endorsements. He wants me to advertise his dumb helmet in a TV commercial."

"What does Manny say about it?"

"He's all for it, of course. I'm the one has to lie about it, but he doesn't care. He thinks I should say it's a good helmet because we'll get TV publicity for the Wheels that way, bring in bigger crowds, make more money."

Randi looked concerned. "The helmet isn't any good?"

"It's a piece of junk."

"Then tell him you won't do the commercial!" She sounded indignant.

"Nah. I'll do it." Jason stood up and gazed out across the ocean. "It's not worth the hassle." He drained the beer can, squeezed it in half, and fired it against the nearby rocks. "Making Manny happy seems to be the name of the game these days."

"Is that how you feel?"

"I don't know. I don't know how I feel." He stood watching the waves foaming against the rocks. A dead fish was floating there, and he watched the waves play with it, sending it out a few feet as they ebbed, and bringing it back as they rolled in again. *That's like me,* he thought. *A poor fish, helpless, tossed around by every force that comes along. Once I thought I could swim on my own, but not now.*

Randi was pressing against his arm, holding it in both of hers. "Remember how happy we were about the team? Remember how we were glad that we could travel together and skate together, and make money at it too? Maybe, if we could keep it up, win that Invitational, you wouldn't have to do anything you didn't want to do anymore."

"How do you figure that?"

"Money. We'll win a share of that twenty thousand dollars. That would solve a lot of problems."

"Yeah, it might at that." He started along the beach, drawing her with him as he walked.

"If we don't win the prize money, the L.A. Wheels probably won't continue as a team," Randi went on, raising her voice against the sea wind that tried to blow it away. "That means we'll have to go back to the way things were."

"Sounds like this race is as important to you as it is to Manny!"

Randi stared at him. "Isn't it important to you?"

He shrugged. "I don't know." That was true, he didn't know. He didn't seem to know what was important these days, and what wasn't. He remembered his dad telling him all the usual things . . . honesty is the best policy . . . be true to yourself . . . don't ever betray a trust. He'd never told him what to do if being honest meant *not* being true to yourself. Randi trusted him; Manny and the other guys on the team trusted him, too. But if he was true to himself, how could he not betray their trust? If he was honest and refused to be in that Yani commercial because he didn't think their helmet was any good, he'd be hurting Manny and the team, and his own chances of making money.

Randi was still standing there with a hurt look on her face. He drew her close to him and held her, laying his cheek against the soft dampness of her hair. He wished he could explain things to her, but how could he when he didn't know what to say? He hugged her instead, and looked out once again at the restless waves, growing dark now as the sun became a thin red line across the horizon. There was such a soft peacefulness out there, when you had a surfboard under you and you knelt on it and waited for a big wave. You could feel like the gulls must feel. No thoughts chasing each other around in your head, but only a watchful, peaceful waiting.

"We'd better go," he told Randi. "You're shivering. It's getting late."

Chapter 19

At 6:30 A.M. Jason and Manny were waiting in the park, Jason wearing his Wheels uniform and a brand-new Day-Glo orange Yani helmet. A few minutes later, a van drove up and disgorged the cameras and crew that were to make the commercial.

Charles Martin was with them. He greeted Manny like a long lost brother, then introduced him and Jason to the director, a slim, balding man with glasses.

The director studied Jason critically. "You're the skateboard star? Can we do something about that hair?" He waved to one of the crew. "George, bring your kit over here. We need a makeup job."

"No makeup," Jason said. He ran his fingers through his hair, feeling self-conscious. "What do you want to do to me? Make me look like Dudley Doright?"

The director appealed to Martin. "How's your helmet going to look on that head of hair?"

Martin turned to Manny. "He's right, Mr.

Bloom. We want to show the Yani helmet to its best advantage, remember."

Manny looked at Jason. "How about it?"

"No way," Jason said firmly. If they started messing with his hair and his face, he was going to walk out. He waited, folding his arms stubbornly.

Manny's face flushed, and for a moment he looked angry. Then, as Jason waited for what he was going to say, he seemed to change his mind. He turned to the director. "If he doesn't want makeup, it's no makeup."

"But Mr. Bloom!" the director wailed.

Martin held up his hands in a peacemaking gesture. "Now, now. The fans are used to seeing Jason this way, and they like him this way. He's a great skater. Great."

Jason let out a sigh of relief. At least Manny was standing up for him, and that was something. But that was only the first of many hassles throughout the morning, and the filming of the commercial, a thirty-second spot, took hours.

The crew broke for lunch and the filming started again afterwards. The director lined Jason up on his marker for the umpteenth time and then went back to stand next to the camera. "Don't look at me," he told Jason. "Talk directly to the camera lens. Everyone ready? Sound? Roll sound."

The production assistant walked in front of Jason, flashing a production plate at the camera. She held it so close to his nose that Jason winced. "Scene three, take eighty-seven," she said.

"Ready now?" the director asked Jason. "Head down . . . second half bumper . . . action."

Jason looked at the camera. "Hi, I'm Jason

Maddox, and I'm wearing here the model 70 Yani helmet—a fantastic helmet. And its . . ."

"Hey, Jason!"

Jason turned at the sound of Brad's voice, and saw that the rest of the team had turned up for the practice session that was supposed to take place after the filming. They were all standing on the sidelines now, watching him.

The director let out a frustrated howl.

Jason looked back into the camera lens. "This Yani helmet is a piece of junk," he said.

He could hear the guys on the team laughing.

Manny hurried over to him. "Hey, Jason, I'm going crazy! This has gone on so long the day will be over and we won't get any practicing in. Could you give them a good commercial and let's get going?"

Jason grinned at him. He could hear the director complaining to Martin, "He blew it again!"

Martin called to Manny, "Mr. Bloom!"

Manny looked at Jason, pleading. "Please, Jason?"

"Sure. The next take will be the last." He reached out as one of the cameramen passed him, carrying two cans of beer, and took one of them.

Manny looked ready to blow up. "Hey, this kid is in training," he told the cameraman. "Don't give him beer!"

"Sorry," the cameraman said, and passed them quickly.

Jason popped the cap of the can and took a quick swallow before Manny took the can out of his hand.

"Look," Martin complained. "The rest of your

team is walking around here with other helmets on. I don't need anybody here with other helmets on!"

"Let's go!" the director called.

"Why do we have these kids here with other helmets on?" Martin asked Manny.

"Stay back, you guys," Manny called to his team. "You're messing up the commercial." He turned to Martin. "I thought these guys said they'd be through by two o'clock?"

"That's what I thought," Martin said.

Manny sounded mad. "Listen, Jason and the rest of my team still got a good three hours' practice to do after this."

Martin nodded and called out to the director. "Try to make it a perfect take this time if you can, Vince. Jason's in training for a big event. We can't tire him out."

"Okay!" the director snapped. "Quiet down everybody. This time I'm serious. I don't want any overlaps, and I want to get this commercial the way it should be. Clean. Now let's go."

The production assistant came in front of Jason again, holding up her production plate. "Scene three, take eighty-eight."

"Good!" The director held up his hand for silence. "Action, Jason."

Jason put on a big smile and looked straight into the blank eye of the camera. "Hi, I'm Jason Maddox. I ride for the L.A. Wheels. My coach wanted me to do this commercial for you. It's a helmet, a fantastic helmet. It's a model 70 Yani, one of the newest, most advanced models on this planet. Believe me, it's unreal." He reached up to the helmet and patted it lovingly. "And for you little kids out there, you know I wouldn't wear it unless it was fantastic."

"That's it!" the director shouted happily. "Loved it! Loved that take! We got it!"

It was late when Jason got back to the beach house. After the commercial, the team had practiced until dark. His brother was there with his girlfriend, and Jason knew they didn't want him hanging around. He took a six-pack of beer from the fridge and drank it in the van, one can right after another, and then went for a drive along the Pacific Coast Highway. But he wasn't driving very well. He couldn't seem to hold the van in a straight line, and after he nearly swerved into an oncoming car, he parked the van by the side of the road. He didn't want to smash up Scott's car. No way.

Through the windshield, the highway stretched dark and smooth and inviting. A perfect place to ride his board. Not a speed bump on it! He laughed and picked his skateboard off the floor where he'd left it, and carried it out to the shoulder of the road. Then he pumped along, trying to build up speed.

There was something wrong, though. He wasn't doing this right. The board just wouldn't behave. He laughed again. What would all his fans say if they saw Jason, their hero, the big wheel of the L.A. Wheels, lumping along like a beginner? Everybody thought Jason could do anything right. He wouldn't ever tell them.

Why was he here, where there were pebbles and grass, when there was a big wide stretch of skating area right beside him? He rode the board out onto the smoothness of the asphalt and centered it on the white line, crouching now to gain speed.

Lights were coming at him. Spotlights. They wanted to see Jason perform. He stretched out his leg into a shoot-the-duck position. There was a loud blast of a horn as the car passed him and Jason smiled. Applause!

But now there were other lights shining on him from both directions, and horns sounding, and brakes screaming. He felt a rush of wind, went off balance, and landed on the roadway. Damn! He couldn't seem to do it right tonight. He checked his elbows for road rash and then got back on his skateboard. Practice. That was the answer. If he practiced hard enough, he'd get it right.

Chapter 20

Manny was sound asleep when the phone rang. He lifted his head and squinted at the clock radio. The digits read 1:45. Could it be Sol calling at this hour? He didn't want to talk to Sol. He lay his head back down on the bed and pulled the pillow over it.

But the ringing wouldn't stop. He was getting a headache from its insistent scream. It wouldn't shut up until he answered it, and he couldn't go back to sleep if it didn't shut up. He reached out a hand, grabbed the receiver, and put it to his ear.

"Hello? Yeah, this is Emanuel Bloom."

What he heard on the other end of the line made him sit straight upright. "What? How long ago? Did you call his brother? I see ... I'll call her. She'll come right up. If there's any problem, I'll call you right back. What's the number?" He switched on the light, looked around for something to write on, found a donut box and a pencil, and wrote on the lid of the box. "Okay. Thank you."

He hung up and rubbed his forehead with his hand, dazed. He reached for the phone again, then looked at the clock and put the receiver back. What should he do? It was late. He'd wake her up. But he had to do it. He picked up the phone again and dialed.

The phone at the other end was picked up quickly, and Millicent's sleepy voice said, "Hello?"

"Millicent, there's a problem. I'm sorry to call you at this hour, but I had to."

"What is it, Manny?" She sounded wide-awake now.

"Jason's been picked up by the Ventura police. His brother can't be reached, and the only one he'll talk to is you. They found him wandering around Pacific Coast Highway, wiped out. The station's straight up One on the Coast Highway, just past Leo Carillo Beach."

"Okay, Manny. I'll go there right away. He's not hurt, is he?"

"No, he's all right. Listen, call me when you find out anything. No, wait. Better still, meet me at the Melting Pot at seven. I'll buy you breakfast."

"Okay, Manny."

"And Millicent . . . thanks. I really appreciate this."

She looked tired and pale when she met him at the Melting Pot, where Manny sat at a table, sipping a bloody mary. She raised her eyebrows when she saw it. "Liquor? At this hour of the morning? Anyway, I thought you didn't drink."

"That's right, I didn't." He didn't add that he hadn't been able to sleep ever since that phone call, and that his nerves were so on edge he hoped a strong drink would calm them. Being Millicent, she would have that already figured out.

She dropped heavily into a chair. "I just took Jason back to his beach house."

"Is everything okay?"

She shrugged. "He seemed confused and tired. He's going to sleep for the rest of the day."

Manny gulped the rest of his drink and set it down hard on the table. "I never planned on anything like this."

"I'm sure nobody did," she said.

Manny felt as though he were going to cry. Guilt, that's what it was. All night he'd been thinking about Jason and Sol and the whole situation.

Millicent covered his hands with hers. "Hey, hey. Take it easy. It's not your fault."

"That's just it. It *is* my fault. It's totally my fault."

"What are you talking about?"

"I'm talking about what *you* talked about the other day. I'm talking about pressure. I'm talking about me making those kids into something that they were never meant to be. I'm talking about—"

Millicent interrupted him. "Hey! How many people can take the blame for the same thing?"

Manny, totally wrapped up in his own misery, didn't understand. "What are you talking about?"

"Jason laid almost the same rap on me. He told me it was all his fault."

"His fault?" Manny shook his head. "How could it be his fault? He's been winning everything, and I was still on his case all the time."

Millicent spoke gently. "You were doing what you thought was best for him and for the team, right?"

Manny signaled a passing waitress. "Would you like a drink?" he asked Millicent, who shook her head. He ordered another for himself. "It's my fault," he went on, "because kids shouldn't have to deal with that kind of pressure. But I thought that the skateboard team would make some fast money for me, and I figured the kids would dig it."

The waitress brought another bloody mary and set it in front of him. Manny took a big swallow.

"Hey," Millicent said, "take it easy!"

Manny stared into his glass. "I know I look like I'd steal from the Salvation Army, but I'd never cheat anybody or try to hand them a raw deal—especially kids."

Millicent covered one of his hands with hers. He looked into her eyes, warm and sympathetic, and he felt lower than a snake's belly. He wanted to crawl away somewhere and hide. But her voice was sincere. "I know you, Manny. I know you aren't like that."

He pulled a handkerchief from his pocket and blew his nose hard. Then he remembered something. "I promised you a breakfast. Here . . ." He handed her the menu the waitress had placed in front of them. "Decide what you want."

"Aren't you eating anything?"

"I'm not hungry."

"I'm a nurse, remember?" she said. "And right at this moment you're my patient. I'm prescribing a good breakfast for you, especially with all that alcohol in you."

She sounded as though she meant business, and he didn't feel like hassling right now. He nodded meekly. After the waitress had taken their order, Millicent lit a cigarette. "I think Jason will be okay," she said. "I told him I'd pick him up tomorrow morning. Let him rest for today. He'll be ready to get to work again tomorrow."

Manny took another sip of his bloody mary. He wondered if Jason would ever want to talk to him again. "I wouldn't count on it," he said.

Chapter 21

Millicent's Porsche glided smoothly along the coast highway. She liked driving by the beach, especially on days like this when the water sparkled, the white birds wheeled, and there was a fresh, salty smell to the air.

She hoped Jason would be feeling better this morning, ready to get back to practicing for the big Downhill Invitational. She knew Manny was ready to apologize to him . . . do his best to let up on the pressure and still have a winning team. She smiled when she thought about Manny. He was a good guy, but he was under a lot of pressure himself, and he passed it on to the team. She found herself liking him a whole lot now that she was learning more about him. One thing for sure, though. He should go on a diet.

The beach house that Jason and Scott shared was a small, brown frame building on the beach, set off by itself. She pulled into the gravel driveway behind the brown van, and got out. It must be great to wake up to the sound of the waves every morning, she thought as she walked down the alley and around to the front of the house.

The man who opened the door in answer to her knock was tall, with red-blond hair like Jason's and a smile like Jason's.

"Hi," Millicent said. "You must be Scott. Jason up yet?"

He looked puzzled. "Are you Randi?"

"Hardly, but thanks for the compliment. I'm Millicent Broderick, the team's nurse. Is he up?"

Scott looked embarrassed. "Jason split real early this morning."

Millicent couldn't believe it. "You mean he's gone?"

Scott nodded. "Come on in. Can I get you a cup of coffee or anything?"

She walked through the door, feeling as though the bottom of the world had dropped away. "No thanks. Where did he go?"

"I don't know. He didn't say. He just said he had to split for a while. The pressure was getting to him."

She nodded slowly. "I was afraid something like this might happen. I really was."

Scott stood in front of the little fireplace. "All he could talk about was the pressure, and, on top of everything else, that commercial really did a number on him."

"Yeah, I should have seen that coming. Manny had a hunch this would happen . . ." She suddenly remembered. Manny! What could she tell him? How was he going to take this?

Scott was still talking. "He's got a lot of things on his mind. He's been trying to figure a way to earn some money—"

"But he can make a lot," Millicent interrupted. "Especially if we can win that prize at the Burbank Invitational."

Scott shrugged. "Let's face it. The Wheels could lose."

Millicent knew he was right, but she couldn't let herself think that. They *had* to win—for Manny's sake, and for everyone else's sake too.

"Will you be seeing Randi?" Scott asked her.

"Yeah, I will. Why?"

"Jason's worried about her, too. She counts on him a lot. He said to tell her he's sorry to leave her like this, but he'll call her when he cools out. He wants her to know he's not gone for good."

"I'll tell her," Millicent said.

The drive back wasn't nearly as pleasant as the drive to the beach had been. Millicent kept trying to figure out how she was going to break the news to Manny and the kids. Manny was as tense as a coiled spring right now, and this might unwind him completely.

She drove the car into the parking area and walked over to the pavement where the team was practicing, Manny pacing nervously as the kids rode their boards in freestyle maneuvers.

Randi skated over to Millicent when she saw her. "Hi," she said casually, but Millicent could see her glancing toward the Porsche as though she hoped Jason might be in it.

"Can I talk to you for a minute?"

"Sure." Randi got off her board and walked a little way to a bench, where both of them sat down.

"I stopped by to pick up Jason this morning. His brother Scott says he's taken off. Seems the pressure got to be too much for him."

Randi looked as though someone had slapped her. Tears started in her eyes, and she blinked to hold them back.

Millicent laid a hand on her arm. "It's going to be all right, Randi. He's not gone for good. Scott said to tell you Jason wanted you to know he's sorry, and that he'll call you soon." She looked up and saw Manny hurrying toward them. "I'm sorry," she told Randi. "I know how you must feel."

Randi looked across the grass at Manny. "He was pushing him too much . . ."

"I know you're upset, but I wouldn't be too hard on Manny. He's only doing what he thinks is best for the team."

"Yeah," Randi said tightly, "but it wasn't right for Jason."

Manny was beside them now, looking anxious. "Where's Jason?"

"He's gone," Millicent said quietly.

"What do you mean, he's gone?" Manny looked from Millicent to Randi, as though one of them might have the answer.

Millicent sighed. "I don't know. I just talked to his brother. He said Jason wanted to have some time alone to get his head together. I wouldn't count on having him around for a while."

Manny's face turned as red as an apple. "It's all my fault. I know it's all my fault."

"No, it isn't. Don't take it personally."

"You know where he is?"

Millicent shook her head. "No, I don't. I just know he'll be back."

"When?"

Randi glared at Manny. "When you learn to stay off his case!"

Manny's face went red, and it was a few seconds before he spoke. "Nobody wants Jason back more than I do, except for you," he told Randi. "I'm really sorry. You've got to believe that. I didn't mean for him to run away."

Randi listened silently, her face hostile.

"You got any idea where he might be?" Manny asked her.

"No."

"Okay." Manny turned to Millicent. "Round up the kids, will you? Get them all over to the bus. We'd better have a meeting."

"Sure." Millicent went to find the others, glad for an excuse to be doing something. The kids were curious about the summons for a meeting, but they went to the bus without too many questions.

Millicent caught Randi's arm as she was about to board the bus. "Let's talk alone for a minute."

"Okay."

They walked a few paces from the bus so the others wouldn't hear them. "What are you going to do?" Millicent asked her.

"About what? Jason?"

"About yourself," Millicent said. "Manny needs you to stay on the team. The other kids will be counting on you. I get the impression you're not too happy with Manny. Maybe since Jason's taken off, you're going to split, too."

Randi's face was stubborn. "Why should I care about Manny? Why should I help him out?"

"You know it's not only Manny. You know what this race means to all of us. You're part of the team."

"So is Jason."

"He said he'd be back, but even if he isn't back for the race, how would it help him if you split, too?"

Randi shook her head. "I don't know, but maybe I will."

Millicent tried again. "Won't you stay with us, Randi, and help the team win?"

The girl stood silently, looking out across the grass.

Manny called to them from the open door of the bus. "Hey, aren't you guys coming?"

"In a minute," Millicent said. She put her hand on Randi's arm. "Well?"

"I don't know," Randi said. "I just don't know."

Chapter 22

I had a hunch Jason had split when Millicent called us to the bus for some mysterious meeting. Word had spread around that something happened to him the other night, and we all figured it had been coming on for a while, even though we didn't know exactly what was going on. I saw Randi and Millicent talking together outside the bus, and saw the look on Randi's face. I wanted to say someting —do something—to make her smile again, but what could I do? So I got on the bus and sat down in one of the front seats.

Manny waited until we were all there, then stuck his head out the door and called to Millicent and Randi. While he waited for them, he groped around in the team's cooler and pulled out a Mountain Dew.

"What's going on?" Tony asked him.

"Tell you in a minute."

"Where's Jason?" Dennis asked from the back.

"Keep cool, Dennis," Manny said, as Randi sat

151

down and Millicent sat down beside her. Then he looked at all of us.

"I'm very upset, and I may not be saying things clearly, but I'd like you to bear with me for a couple of minutes. All right? We don't have Jason anymore. He's gone away for a while."

Everybody talked at once, asking questions. "Where did he go?" "What happened?" "Will he be back for the big race?"

Manny held up his hands for silence. "I don't know. He just split for a few days." He looked unhappy and bewildered, as though he couldn't understand what happened or why, but all of us could understand.

Most of us who like skateboarding are pretty much loners. We don't want to have coaches or managers telling us how to skate. That's why we choose skateboarding as our sport instead of things like baseball or soccer. Each one of us is alone on his skateboard, even with a team, and he can be as creative as he wants with the skills his body has acquired. He sets his own limits according to what he knows he can do.

Manny hadn't tried to tell any of us how to do our freestyle tricks, or anything like that, but he had been pushing us to practice, pushing us to get in top shape, and he had pushed Jason into doing things *his* way. Jason was probably the most alone of this whole team of loners, and he knew how good he was. You don't order Picasso to paint you a landscape, or tell the Beatles to write the music for a TV commercial.

Somehow I didn't mind that Jason had split, even though I knew he'd miss a lot of practice. He was our contestant for the big downhill race, and he had to be in good shape for it. I was more worried about Randi, hoping that she wasn't going to split, too.

She was sitting there next to Millicent, her face frozen in a look that was half-sad, half-angry, watching Manny with big, shiny eyes. "Why don't you tell them *why* he split, Manny?" she said.

He turned red and shouted at her, "I don't know why! He just split, that's all! What do you want from me?"

Everyone stopped talking, and I could feel the tension in the air as we waited silently to see what was going to happen.

Manny gave in. He slumped against the dashboard of the bus and his face got red. "All right, I'm sorry. I didn't mean to holler at you. That's probably why Jason took off. Maybe it was my fault . . . the pressure and everything. So I admit I was wrong."

I liked Manny better at that moment than I'd ever liked him, and I think the others did too. The tension relaxed and I could hear somebody popping bubble gum, while somebody else behind me spun his skateboard wheels.

"Randi, I've got to ask you a favor," Manny went on. "You probably don't owe me this—I mean, I know how you feel—but I hope you'll stay with the team."

She looked as though she'd been considering that for a while. She frowned and twisted her fingers together in the silence. Then she looked up and nodded. "All right."

Manny smiled with relief. "That means a great deal to me, no kidding."

Millicent reached for Randi's hand and I could

see her squeeze it, and say "good for you" in a low voice. I was just as happy as they were. The team wouldn't have been the same without her.

But something else was bothering me. It sounded, the way Manny and Randi were talking, as though Jason wasn't going to come back. I knew Manny had said he was going for "a few days," so why all the big deal? I was even more worried when Manny quieted all the chatter that had broken out and gave us his next shocker.

"Now," he said, "I need somebody to take Jason's place."

We all looked at each other, surprised, and Peter said, "Nobody could do that!"

Tony leaned back in his seat and put his feet up on the back of the seat ahead. "You've flipped out!" he told Manny.

"How about you? You could do the downhill race," Manny said.

"Why? Isn't Jason coming back to do it himself?"

"It's only ten days away," Manny said. "I hope he'll be back, but I'm not sure. So I'm going to have to rely on you for that one."

"But I'm not into the downhill!" Tony objected. "It's not my thing. I'm into slalom, not downhill."

"You can do both the slalom and the downhill, okay?"

"Why don't you get Brad to do it?" Tony said. "He's into the downhill more than I am. He likes it, too."

I couldn't race the downhill! I was nowhere near as good as Jason! Everyone started talking all at once, telling Manny I was the one to do it; telling me to take over for Jason. They sounded crazy to me.

Manny seemed doubtful. "Brad's half your size, Tony—" he began, but Tony wasn't listening. He was talking to me.

"You can do it! Right, Brad?"

Randi was looking past Millicent, straight at me. The look had hope in it, and a kind of admiration. She wanted me to say yes. Winning that Burbank race must mean a lot to her, so why would she want me to do it? Maybe she realized that if Jason didn't come back in time to race the downhill, he'd be letting the team down pretty badly. Maybe she was counting on me to come through . . . for her and for Jason.

Millicent leaned toward me across the aisle. "Can you do it, Brad?"

"I'm years away from being as hot as Jason," I said.

Manny sounded confident. "Hey, I don't want to hear stuff like that. You've got the ability to be as hot as any skater around."

Randi was still looking that look at me. "Don't put yourself down, Brad."

What could I do? "All right," I told them. "I'll do it."

Manny grinned and everyone seemed happy about my decision.

"We'll help you all we can," Peter told me.

"You can do it, Brad," Jenny called.

"I hope so," I said.

Manny was suddenly all business. "All right, we've got that settled. You girls will have to come first in every event in Burbank. We won't have any points to spare. We don't have any more time to spare, either, so let's get out there and practice. Everybody out!"

As the others piled off the bus, he grabbed my arm. "I'll work with you, Brad," he said, "but I won't get on your case. Don't worry about that. I'll just work hard with you, okay?"

"I'll work hard too," I told him, "but—"

He brushed away my objections with a wave of his hand. "No more negative thinking. It's positive from now on."

"Okay," I said.

In the days that followed I did work hard, but I was scared. I didn't like taking Jason's place, having everyone counting on me to win that downhill race and the twenty thousand dollars' prize money. I kept thinking about that time in Little League when everyone had counted on me to strike those batters out, and I'd let them make a home run. I'd been so nervous I'd just gone to pieces and forgotten everything I knew about pitching. I was afraid the same thing would happen in the downhill race.

And I didn't believe the other kids on the team thought I could win. I think they all believed Jason would turn up in time for the race. I hoped he would, so I would get off the hook, but the days passed and there was no word from him. Nobody seemed to know where he was, not even Randi.

In the meantime, I tried to build up my speed, practicing the crouching position with my arms forward which creates a foil to break the body's resistance to the wind, and learning to flow into the turns. Downhill racing is dangerous, though, be-

cause of the high speed of the skaters and the
chance that hitting a bump on the course or shift-
ing your position carelessly can topple you off your
board and cause serious injury. If you fall on a
hard surface going thirty or forty miles an hour, it
can get pretty hairy. I had to be very sure I knew
what I was doing every minute.

Manny pushed me as hard as he had been
pushing Jason, but at least I could understand why.
He was trying to turn me into another Jason in ten
days. It wasn't working. There were only two days
left now until the Burbank Invitational, and I
hadn't come near Jason's speed. I'd been able to
cut five seconds off my time since yesterday,
though, and Manny seemed pleased about that.

I was taking a break, sitting on a bench beside
the slope, when Jenny and Randi passed me on
their skateboards, going fast. When Randi saw me
she crouched, put her hands on the ground, and
pivoted in a power slide that brought her to a stop.
Jenny kept on going, her blonde curls flying under
her helmet.

Randi came over and sat on the bench beside
me. "I'm tired," she said. "Think I'll rest for a
while."

I felt happy and awkward all at once. She was
paying a lot more attention to me these days, but I
wasn't as brave in real life as I'd been in my daydreams about her. I still felt shy and clumsy when-
ever she was around.

She took her gloves off and removed her helmet,
shaking her hair so that it fell around her face.
"How's it going?" she asked me.

"Fine. Have you ... uh ... have you heard
from Jason?"

She looked at me sadly. "No. Have you?"

"No. Why would he call me?" I looked down at my sneakers. "I just thought maybe he'd called you. Maybe he's coming back."

"In time for the race, you mean?" She didn't sound very confident. "I think he'll be back any time now. He knows when it is."

She didn't make me believe her, and I could tell she was hurt that he hadn't called her. I tried to make her feel better. "Maybe he's not near a phone."

"Yeah," she said. "Maybe." She reached out suddenly and put her hand on my arm. "What's bugging you, Brad? You worried about the race?"

"No way," I told her, sounding as positive as I could. "I just cut five seconds off yesterday's time."

"That's great!"

"Yeah," I said, and reached to take her hand. It felt soft and warm in mine. "Come on, let's get something to drink."

I was afraid if we sat there any longer I'd let it slip how scared I was, and how rotten I was going to feel when the L.A. Wheels lost the Burbank Downhill Invitational, and twenty thousand dollars, because of me.

Chapter 23

Randi was washing the dishes the night before the competition while her nine-year-old sister Chrissie, who was supposed to be drying them, watched TV in the family room next to the kitchen.

Dinner that night had been worse than usual. Her dad hadn't come home from the office, and her mom, upset about it, had started in on Randi about the Wheels again.

"Skateboards, Randi! That's kid stuff. You're almost eighteen and you should be acting like a lady instead of a tomboy."

"Lots of girls like skateboarding, Mom," Randi told her patiently for at least the hundredth time.

Her mother put a finger to her lips. "Sssh! Listen! Is that your dad's car in the driveway?"

"Naw," Chrissie said. "It's next door."

"Oh. Well, isn't this team you belong to mostly boys?"

"There's one other girl. Jenny Bradshaw." Randi poked her fork around in her spinach. She didn't like spinach. It seemed they had spinach seven

159

nights a week. Why didn't Jason call her? What was he doing? Was he all right?

"What is this big event going on tomorrow?" her mother asked.

"It's a competition, Mom. Skateboarding competition. There's a big prize. Lots of money. If we win, we'll split it up among the members of the team." She'd told her parents the same thing before, but neither of them seemed to remember. Her mother wasn't really listening to her now. She was listening for the sound of her husband's car, worried that he'd stopped at some bar on the way home. Randi had long ago stopped worrying whether or not her dad would be sober when he got home. It happened so seldom. She'd learned just to get out of her parents' way at the first sign of an argument. At least tonight her mother wasn't drinking, but Randi didn't like to see her so white-faced and nervous. Maybe if she did take a drink she'd look happier.

"Why don't you take up something like tennis or swimming?" her mother asked her. "Much more suitable for a girl your age."

"Because I can't win tennis matches or swimming meets, Mom. I'm better at skateboarding, and the L.A. Wheels is a pro team."

Her mother put a hand to her forehead. "I've got an awful headache. I think I'll lie down for a while."

"Can I go over to Linda's to do my homework?" Chrissie asked.

"All right. After you help Randi with the dishes. Be home by nine o'clock." She stood up. "And Randi, you'd better not mention to your father that you're still on that team. You know he gets upset about it."

"Okay, Mom." Randi began to clear the dishes off the table. Her father got upset about most things, so what else was new?

After her mother had gone to her bedroom and Chrissie had plopped herself down in front of the TV, Randi washed the dishes quickly. She was tired. Today's practice had been pretty strenuous, but she'd finally got that backwards flip down perfect, landing on one skateboard, then rolling to another one placed a short distance away, and doing a forward flip onto that. Everyone said it was a great trick.

She wasn't worried much about the freestyle events; it was Brad doing that downhill that worried her. He was good, but he didn't seem to have any confidence in himself, and of course he wasn't Jason. She liked him a lot, but he just wasn't Jason.

Still, he had to win that downhill. She was counting on the money. Everybody was. For a while she'd thought the money would enable her and Jason to go away together, but now she wasn't so sure that's what she wanted. She knew she still liked Jason a lot, but something in their relationship had changed when he went away without saying anything to her or even phoning her to let her know he was going. If he could leave her and leave the team just like that, she wasn't sure she could trust him as much as she used to. Maybe Millicent was right. Maybe Randi should get her own head on straight . . . decide what she wanted to do with her life . . . instead of pinning all her hopes and dreams on Jason.

When the phone in the family room rang, Chrissie ran to pick it up before Randi could get to it. Then she held it out, pulling a face. "It's for you. Guess who?"

It was Jason.

"Where are you?" Randi asked him.

"At the beach."

"At home?"

"No. I haven't gone home yet." His voice sounded distant. "How're you doing?"

"Better, now that I've heard from you. We've all been worried."

"Sweetie pie," Chrissie whimpered. "Darling. Lover boy." She settled herself on the arm of a chair and cupped a hand around her ear to show she was listening.

"Go watch TV," Randi told her, but Chrissie just stayed where she was.

"What have you been doing?" Randi asked Jason.

"Nothing much," he said. "Mostly just nothing."

"You going to make it for the downhill tomorrow?"

There was a long pause, then his voice came, reluctantly. "I guess so. I guess I better make it."

"Don't you *want* to?"

She could hardly hear him, he was speaking so softly. "I still feel pretty wigged out, but I'll be there."

"That's great," she said. "We talked Brad into taking your place in case you didn't come back in time, but he's scared."

"Brad?" His voice got stronger. "Yeah, Brad can do it."

"He can't, Jason. He's too scared."

"That's his trouble. He's got no confidence. He figures I'm the hot one. They all do. But Brad's good . . . real good. He can win the downhill."

"Jason!" Randi's voice was a wail.

Chrissie echoed it. "Jason baby! Jason darling! Jason sweetie!"

Randi shot her a murderous look. She'd get her later, after the phone call.

Chrissie seemed to get the message. She left the room in a hurry.

"You've got to come back, Jason!"

"No. Listen, I'm no hero."

Randi felt a pang of deep disappointment. *"I'm* counting on you." she said.

There was another moment of silence, and she wondered whether he'd heard her. Then he said, "This will be the best thing for Brad."

He must have heard her! He just didn't want to be *her* hero either. She wanted to cry, but she didn't want him to hear her. "What if Brad loses?" she asked him.

"What if *I* lose? See, that really gets me. Nobody seems to think I could lose. I could!"

She tried to protest again, but he cut her off. "This is long distance, baby. I don't have that much bread. Just don't say anything to anybody that I called. I'll be seeing you soon."

Chapter 24

Manny, too, got a phone call the night before the Burbank race.

He was too nervous to sleep—he'd been like this for days now—so he was lying in bed watching an old movie on late-night TV, only half-aware of what the actors were doing on the screen, a can of Mountain Dew in his hand and some donuts on the night table beside him.

The ringing of the phone startled him, so that he splashed his drink across the front of his pajama top. It felt cold on his skin underneath. He muttered miserably to himself and tried to pull off the wet top, but as the phone rang insistently he gave up the attempt and picked it up.

"Hello, Manny." It was Sol. "How are your kids doing?"

Manny forced a cheerful note into his voice. "Oh, terrific . . . just terrific, Sol! They're all in great shape."

"So we'll be square after tomorrow, right?"

"Oh yeah, you can count on it, Solly. You'll

have ten grand by three o'clock tomorrow afternoon." Manny felt sweat trickling down his forehead.

"I'm glad to hear you sound so confident, Manny."

"I sure am. We're all confident, me and the team. We sure are." His mouth felt dry as he said it. He took another sip of his drink.

Sol's voice went on, sounding friendly. "You know, Manny, I bet we would both sleep a lot better tonight if we knew what was going to happen tomorrow."

"What do you mean, Sol? We do know what's going to happen."

"I'll bet you'd really sleep better if you knew that you were going to be square with me and have thirty grand ahead."

"What are you talking about?" Manny, in his surprise, forgot to sound cheerful.

"Thirty thousand dollars is what I'm talking about."

"You mean you're going to give me four-to-one odds?"

"I'm not talking about a bet, idiot!"

"Then what *are* you talking about?"

Sol was silent for a moment before he spoke again. "The final race. The one worth double points . . ."

"The downhill? What about it?"

"Have the kid take a dive."

"Dive? What do you mean?"

"You know what I mean. Have the kid fall down, nice and easy, near the end. You do me that favor and I'll make a killing on what I'm betting. I'll do you a favor and pay you forty thousand out of my winnings. You give me ten grand of that, you get thirty grand under the table that nobody knows about, and everybody's happy."

The suggestion gave Manny a cold chill. For a moment he couldn't believe what Sol had said; then he did believe it, and wanted to hang up the phone.

And then he felt another emotion ... a great sense of relief. There would be no more need to worry about the race. The outcome would be all settled before it ever began! No need to worry about Jason being gone, and Brad turning chicken or not being good enough. No need to worry about what would happen to him if he didn't have ten thousand dollars to pay Sol. He'd have that much and thirty thousand extra! Wouldn't that be the solution to all of their problems ... not only his, but the kids' too.? They'd have more money to share if they lost the race!

But what about all the practicing and hard work? Well, that hadn't hurt anyone, had it? How much did it mean if they won a skateboarding competition, anyway? He knew the team was great, and they *were* great, so what did a race or two prove?

"Well?" Sol asked impatiently.

"Manny hesitated, still thinking fast. "Well ..."

He remembered then. He remembered Dennis practicing three-sixties that day, and how happy he'd been because he could do them faster and keep them up longer than anybody else on the team. He remembered Jenny, doing her hand-stands and arabesques as gracefully as any ballet dancer. He thought of Peter and Tony working out their new routine—the one they'd finally perfected this morning. Their timing had been something to see. He remembered how Randi had stayed with the team and worked hard after Jason left, and how happy Manny had been about her staying. And Brad, who'd practiced so faithfully these last few days, even though he was so worried about taking Jason's place. Manny remembered Jason, too. That spaced-out kid who could skate like a gust of wind. He could see them all in his head, and Millicent was there too—Millicent, who had held his hand softly and always been there when he needed her. They were all waiting to hear what he'd say.

They helped him give Sol his answer.

"We've got no deal, Sol."

"No deal, huh?" Sol's voice made Manny think of a shark, waiting in murky water. "You mean you won't have your kid take a dive?"

"That's right. I won't. We're going to win tomorrow."

Sol didn't want to give up. "Manny, nobody would have to know."

"*I'd* know," Manny said. "My team would know."

The shark opened its jaws. "Okay, Manny. You'd better win. You're betting your life. Remember that." The phone clicked into ominous silence.

Manny sat with the phone in his hand, feeling numb. "I've got to be crazy," he told himself. "I just turned down forty thousand dollars? I just told Sol to get lost? I've got to be out of my mind." The phone began to hum and he hung it up. "Brad's got to win that race tomorrow. He's going to. Because if he doesn't . . ."

The shark in his thoughts closed its jaws, and the murky water turned bloody.

Chapter 25

The park was crowded with people on the day of the Burbank Downhill Invitational. Tiers of benches had been set up along the slope where the races were held, and although they were filled, spectators were still arriving. The preliminary races had been going on all morning. Jenny and Tony were to be finalists in the slalom races, and Brad had qualified for the final downhill race.

Jenny, seated beside Tony on one of the benches reserved for the competing teams, squinted in the sunlight and tried to see if Jason might be somewhere in the crowd.

Tony finished checking the wheels of his skateboard, put his T-bar in his pocket, and looked up. "You find him?"

"No. Do you think he'll show up?"

Tony shrugged. "Who knows? Look at all these people coming to see the L.A. Wheels win the big one!"

"We hope."

"Positive thinking, like Manny says." Tony held

up his skateboard, checking its surface.

"No way. This is my good old hickory slalom special." Tony scraped a speck of dirt from its edge with his fingernail. "All tuned up and ready to win."

There was a slight, warm breeze that made the pennants on the field flutter; kids were squealing and calling to each other, and Jenny could feel the excitement that hummed through the park.

She wasn't really worried. Randi, Dennis, and Peter had made points in the freestyle event that had been held earlier, Tony seemed relaxed and confident, and she was going to do her best in the girls' slalom. That's all anybody could do. But she was concerned about Brad. He'd been very quiet all day, and she wondered what he was thinking.

Dennis came up to her, carrying hot dogs and canned drinks in a cardboard box. "Here," he said, shoving a hot dog and a soda at her. "Manny told me to bring you these."

"How about me, man?" Tony reached out for his share.

Dennis pulled the carton to his chest. "Manny says you get something to eat after you race, not before."

"Jenny hasn't raced yet," Tony complained.

"Her race doesn't start for a while. Manny says it's okay for her but not for you."

Tony took a deep sniff of the hot dogs, and Dennis turned and ran to the bench where Peter was waiting. He sat down and shared the contents of the box.

"Will you show me how to do that trick you did with Tony?" he asked Peter.

"You can't do it. You're too short." Peter bit into his hot dog and watched the crowds.

"How come I'm always too young or too short?"

"Never mind," Peter said. "You'll get older and taller. Everybody does. Did you see Jason anywhere?"

"No. Do you think Brad can win the downhill?"

"Sure he can," Peter said.

"How come you didn't take Jason's place instead of him?"

"I didn't want to. I like freestyle." Peter took another bite. "Besides, I guess we all thought Jason would be back with the team by now." He glanced over at Brad, sitting beside Randi. He sure looked scared.

Brad checked the trucks of his skateboard, making sure the locknuts and the action bolts were tight.

Randi laughed at him. "They've got to be perfect by now, you've checked them so often."

"Yeah?" Brad smiled, trying not to show his nervousness.. "Well, all I need is to drop my wheels coming down that slope."

"Hey, you're a cinch to win," Randi told him. "Even Jason said so."

He stared at her. "When did Jason say that? How did he know I'm racing the downhill?"

"He phoned me last night," Randi said. "I shouldn't have let that slip. He asked me not to say anything to anybody."

"He's not going to be here today?"

She shook her head. "I don't know. He said he'd see me soon."

"Great," Brad said bitterly. So Jason knew, and

still he didn't care that they might lose the race.

"He said he still felt pretty wigged out," Randi said defensively. "He doesn't want to let the team down. He just feels you can win."

Brad felt a sudden anger—at Jason, for dropping out like this; at Randi for defending him; at Manny and the rest of the guys for putting him in this position, where he didn't want to be.

The announcer's voice was coming over the speakers, and the crowd hushed to hear him. "Will all skaters who have reached the finals report to the officials' stand."

Brad got up and began walking toward the tables set up by the slope where the races would be. The race officials were already seated there, pads and pencils in front of them. He felt lightheaded, as though this wasn't really happening to him. He wanted to walk right past the officials, across the grass and out of the park, but there was no escape for him. He had to go through with it. He passed Manny and Millicent, standing together, and Manny clapped a hand on his shoulder as he passed.

"Nice going in those qualifying runs," Manny said.

Brad nodded and tried to smile, but his mouth felt stiff.

Manny watched him walking toward the officials. "He'll do okay," he told Millicent.

"Sure he will." Millicent smiled at him.

The loudspeakers blared. "The warm-up ramps will close in ten minutes. The afternoon finals are about to begin."

Millicent could see Tony and Jenny standing with Brad, talking with the officials. Now Tony was leaving, skateboard in hand, going up the hill where the slalom would be run.

"How are we doing so far?" she asked Manny.

He clutched a can of Mountain Dew in one shaking hand. "We did pretty good in the freestyle, but we need every point we can get."

"Ladies and gentlemen," the announcer said. "We hope you've enjoyed the preliminary races at professional skateboarding's biggest competition, the Burbank Downhill Invitational. The first event will be the men's slalom."

"That's Tony's race," Millicent said. She looked up to the top of the hill, recognizing Tony's bright green-and-yellow uniform. His opponents were from the California Rainbow Team, in red and blue, the Duraflex team, in dark green and white and the Suns team, in red, white and blue.

The crowd noises died to a murmur as everyone watched the racers.

"They're off!" the announcer called. "Tony Bluetile of the L.A. Wheels has just jumped into a big lead!"

The two skateboarders raced down the slope, curving in and out between the slalom cones.

"Keep those turns tight!" Manny shouted.

The California Rainbower was gaining, Millicent saw, and her hand tightened on Manny's arm. Now he was in the lead! But Tony was coming up fast, skating smoothly and confidently, flowing between the cones with ease until he had passed him by two . . . no, three cones.

Nearing the finish line, the Sims skateboarder caught up and the two swerved and swooped together like flying gulls, then Tony suddenly moved ahead and streaked across the finish line.

Manny whooped with joy, and Millicent flung her arms around his neck, shrieking happily. The crowd was roaring. Tony came toward them, popping a bubble, grinning all over his face, and the other team members ran up and clapped him on the back, congratulating him. The Wheels had won the first slalom!

The voice of the announcer resounded through the loudspeakers. "It's Bluetile of the Wheels, winning the men's giant slalom. The next event will be the women's giant slalom. This race will be run over a quarter-of-a-mile course. There will be a few moments delay while the girls go through their technical safety inspection."

Jenny took off the straw hat she'd been wearing, plopped it onto Dennis's head as she passed him, and fastened her helmet under her chin.

"Get going, kid," Manny told her.

"Good luck!" Millicent called.

Jenny smiled at both of them and went toward the officials.

"There will be six contenders in the women's slalom race, ladies and gentlemen," the announcer said. "Jenny Bradshaw, Robin Logan, Laura Thornhill, Edie Robertson, Rebecca Williams, and Robin Allaway. The racers will be ready to start in a moment."

There was a man coming toward them, pressing past the benches where team members sat watching. The man was looking more intent on Manny than he was on the race that was about to begin. Millicent suddenly felt afraid.

The man walked over to Manny. "Sol wants to

have a little talk with you."

Manny stuck his hands in his jacket pockets and gave the man a cold stare. "He does, huh?"

"Yeah."

"You tell him to get lost. Tell him I'm too busy right now."

The man ran his fingers through his thinning, greasy hair. "You really want me to tell him that?"

"Yeah," Manny said. "Why don't you?"

"All right." The man turned and walked away.

Millicent couldn't understand Manny's changed attitude. The man had obviously been one of the same crowd who'd beaten Manny up, but Manny hadn't seemed to be the least afraid of him. What had happened? Was Manny that sure of winning the prize money? But now the announcer's voice was telling them the race had begun, and Jenny and the others were starting down the slope. Millicent turned to watch.

The racers looked about even, but now Jenny seemed to be pulling ahead of the bunch. Millicent squeezed her hands together and wished hard. *Come on, Jenny! We need the points you can win! I'm not sure what's going on with Manny, but there's somebody here waiting to eat him alive if we don't win the prize, so Jenny . . . give it all you've got!*

Jenny was still ahead, winding swiftly between the cones, her body balancing gracefully on the skateboard. She was keeping close to the cones, Millicent saw, to cut down the distance she had to travel. Now she was too close! The cone was toppling and her skateboard seemed to be veering out of control! She was losing her balance!

Jenny struggled to right herself, but as the

skateboard swerved off at an angle to the course, she tumbled off it, went into a rolling fall as she hit the pavement, and then slowly picked herself up and walked to the grassy shoulder.

Millicent grabbed her medical kit and ran toward her. She could hear the announcer as she ran. "Oh, oh! Bradshaw's down. Now she's getting up, ladies and gentlemen. She doesn't seem to be injured, but Robertson has opened up the lead. Robin Logan is closing and challenging, taking over the lead now . . ."

Millicent knelt on the grass beside Jenny. "You aren't hurt, are you?"

Jenny shook her head, looking pale and dazed. Her left thigh was scraped and bleeding.

Millicent opened her kit, hearing Manny's voice behind her.

"You hurt bad?"

"It's just an abrasion," Millicent said.

Jenny shook her head sadly. "I couldn't help it. I'm sorry."

"I know you couldn't help it." Manny knelt beside her. "You were doing exactly the right thing. It was just bad luck, that's all."

Millicent pulled out antiseptic and began dabbing it on the wound. "At least you know how to take a fall. Rolling into it like that saved you from breaking bones.

Other members of the team were gathering around Jenny, comforting her, talking all at once. Millicent finished binding the wound and looked up at Manny. "Well, what do you think? Are we still in the lead?"

"Do I think we're still in the lead? Are you kidding?" He sounded nervous, upset, and irritable.

Millicent tried a soothing tactic. "We've got a chance to win with Brad, haven't we?"

Jenny watched both of them sadly. "It's my fault."

Manny helped her up. "Will you stop talking like that? You skated a great race there, kid. It's just the breaks."

They got Jenny back to the benches and sat her down on one of them.

The announcer spoke. "The men's downhill race is for double points. The team prize is still up for grabs. And now, on this beautiful summer Saturday, we're just about set for the final and greatest event, the one-mile downhill."

Brad was standing with Randi close by, and Manny turned to him and grabbed him by the arm. "Look me in the eyes," he said. "Who's going to win?"

"I am," Brad said.

"You bet you are." Manny thumped his arm and let it go. "Keep your head on straight!"

"I'm a little scared," Brad said. "One of those guys I'm racing against threatened me."

"Don't worry about them," Manny said. "Can't you take a little threat?" He poked a finger against the chest of Brad's new uniform. "Know how much I paid for this leather outfit?" (Manny had paid $450 for the green and yellow outfit with "L.A. Wheels" emblazoned on front and back.)

"Yeah," Brad said.

"Remember? All right. Make it worth it." Manny turned to Millicent. "Give him a kiss for luck."

Millicent kissed Brad, and then Randi put her

arms around his neck and kissed him too.

Millicent had noticed that Randi seemed to be getting fond of Brad now that Jason wasn't here, and Brad seemed to love it. Well, that might be good for everyone. Jason would find out he couldn't walk away and expect everything to be the same when he came back. Randi would find out there were other people in the world besides Jason, and Brad would get a little more self-confidence from all the attention she was giving him. Or was she just trying to help him win the race in the only way she knew how?

They all listened to the announcer. "There are eight entrants for the downhill race, one from each team in contention for the twenty thousand dollars' grand prize money. The racers are Lance Smith of the Road Runners, Russ Gosnell of Tracker Trucks, John Hughes of Powerpaw, Mike Williams from Doleway, Bob Madrigal from Brewer, Craig Chaquico from the Starship team, Brad Logan of Logan Earthski team, and a new entrant, replacing Jason Maddox . . . Brad Harris for the Los Angeles Wheels."

The crowd applauded and cheered, and the announcer waited for the noise to die before he went on. "This event will start in exactly fifteen minutes. The Pro-Am Racing Association Inspectors are now . . ."

Manny spoke to Brad. "Get over there, kid!"

They watched him go, Millicent thinking how many hopes were going with him. Brad now had the power to change all their lives, and in the next half-hour they'd know whether the change would be for the better or not. Manny's very life depended on Brad, and maybe Millicent's did too; for if something happened to Manny she knew her life would never be the same.

The team members were back on their benches, and she and Manny were standing by themselves, away from the crowd, when she saw the man again. This time he was with another man, and the two were coming toward them. This other man must be Sol, Millicent realized. The Sol who had wanted to see Manny earlier.

Manny saw them too. "You'd better go," he told her. "I don't want you mixed up with these guys." He walked over to meet them, and Millicent stayed where she was. She didn't care if she was eavesdropping. She wanted to be close by in case Manny needed her.

Sol and his friend didn't even glance her way.

"What's all this about, Manny?" Sol looked very angry, puffing furiously at a long, black cigar. "You don't want to see me, or are you too busy to see me?"

"I'm not too busy to see you, Solly. Just don't send this punk around. I'm trying to get your ten grand. Just leave me alone."

"Who's that little putz you're putting in the race?"

"The little putz who's going to win your ten grand back."

Ten thousand dollars? Millicent couldn't believe it. No wonder Manny was so worried. That was a lot of money!

Sol's voice was loud and impatient. "I want to know what happened to Jason—what's his name? —Maddox?"

"He skipped on me, Sol. He flew the coop a few days ago."

"He disappeared? Why didn't you tell me about it?"

"I got another kid," Manny said patiently. "He's going to win."

Sol sounded disgusted. "You got a little kid that can't win anything."

"He'll win. You'll get your ten grand back. I swear it."

Millicent could tell how nervous Manny was. His voice sounded shaky.

Sol waved his cigar in Manny's face. "You listen to me, prune belly. I've been supporting you for a long time, and now you put in this little kid to win this race?"

"He's going to win. I've been working with him for the last ten days."

"All right. Then why didn't you tell me about this kid?"

"Because I didn't want him to take a dive either. He's not going to lose. I swear he'll win!"

Sol's voice dropped to a menacing growl. "Manny, I've got to have my ten grand."

"You'll get it, I swear you will. I've never lied to you, man!"

"Shut up and listen! If I don't get that ten grand, you're dead!"

"Okay." Manny accepted this threat calmly. "But now I'm alive, right? I've still got some time. And you're going to have your ten grand. We're going to win this race."

The loudspeakers were sending the announcer's voice through the park. "All right, ladies and gentlemen, the racers have just passed the technical inspection and we're ready, on this beautiful day, for the exciting final event of downhill racing."

Chapter 26

I was nervous at the starting line, knowing I was going to have to go through with this . . . knowing there was no way out now.

The guys I was competing against were lined up with me. They all looked at least a couple of years older and twenty pounds heavier than me. I felt like a midget, sandwiched between the two biggest, John Hughes and Lance Smith.

I looked down the slope. There was Manny, with Millicent beside him, waving at me. And there was Randi, smiling encouragement. The others must be too far away to see, but I knew they were pulling for me and that helped a lot. One thing I'd done was ask my folks not to come today. It had been easy to persuade them. They still thought that skateboarding, especially downhill racing, was dangerous, although when they learned I'd promised to take Jason's place they didn't try to talk me out of it. I was glad they weren't there. I still remembered that Little League game, and how I'd let them down so badly. I didn't want to go through that again. Whatever happened, I wouldn't have to face their disappointment, anyway.

The timing lights were on. I tensed, watching for the starting signal. When it came, I fumbled with my board and made a clumsy start, and then I saw that the others were all ahead of me. I was alone at the back of the bunch.

I turned my body slightly to lower the wind resistance and felt myself gathering speed. Now I was passing the last man, then the next, and then the two ahead who were running neck and neck. I was even with Craig now, but John and Lance were still far ahead of us, skating close together. Then I saw that Lance was leaning toward John, trying to elbow him off his board. John swayed, then caught his balance and threw his right shoulder slightly to the right, bracing himself for another push, but Lance sent another, harder shove at him and this time John lost his balance and fell. He rolled onto the grass, but he was out of the race.

The tussle between these two had slowed them, and now I was catching up with Lance. I glanced quickly over my shoulder and saw that the other racers were a good distance behind us, and we were leading the pack, speeding down the slope at breakneck speed. If I could get past this guy, I'd have it made!

But as I came up beside him, Lance leaned toward me and nudged. I saw it coming and tensed to meet it, but my board wobbled and I lost speed. I could feel a hot rush of anger. "Try that again!" I shouted, closing in on him.

The big guy gave me a menacing grin over his shoulder. "Stay back, puny!"

This cheater wasn't going to win! If it took everything I had, I was going to beat this guy! I crouched, putting all my concentration into catching up with him and passing him, leaning into the curves in the course, gathering speed until I got up beside him on the same side John had.

That was all Lance needed. He blocked me hard, and for a moment my board zoomed crazily and the world blurred before my eyes. I could feel myself toppling, and for a microsecond I thought I was going to fall, until suddenly I was balancing again. I was still right on Lance's tail, and the finish line was only seconds away from us. I could hear Manny's voice, and Tony's, rising above the roar of the crowd, cheering me on, trusting me, counting on me.

Counting on me! I suddenly thought of the Little League game again. I could almost hear Dad's voice cheering me on from the bleachers. I felt the same panic I felt then—the same doubts. My legs began to shake. I couldn't do it! This big guy was going to win!

But this time I was angry. That cheater *wasn't* going to win! The Little League game had happened a long time ago, and it wasn't going to haunt me the rest of my life. I leaned hard into the wind, stretched my arms out, palms together, and went speeding forward until I was almost level with Lance and could see him tensing to shove me again. I crouched lower so that the nudge missed me, and then I was out in front—alone—and the finish line was just ahead of me.

I was past it! The Wheels had won! The crowd shouted it . . . photographers flashed pictures of it . . . the announcer broadcasted it to the world!

"Brad Harris of the L.A. Wheels has won the

Burbank Downhill Invitational!"

I can't believe it! Is that really my name they announced as the winner? My head was spinning with excitement.

Excited spectators were all around me, clapping my back, shaking my hand, hugging me. Now I could see Manny and Millicent trying to get through the crowd, and Jenny, Tony, Peter, Dennis, and Randi were suddenly surrounding me, all of them laughing and cheering. They wouldn't let me go, so it was a long time before Manny could lead me through the throng toward a stage that had been set up near the finish line, where several official-looking people were waiting.

"I knew you could do it!" Manny told me as we went.

That was strange. Manny knew I could do it, but I hadn't known I could. I'd made up my mind to try, but I never thought I'd win. That must mean I didn't know myself very well, that I didn't know what I could do if I tried. Maybe wanting it badly enough was the answer. Maybe if you wanted to do something strongly enough and worked hard enough for it, you could do it. I'd remember that.

The high school band was playing something loud and cheerful. Manny and I went up the stairs to the stage where a bearded man in a western shirt stood waiting for us, and a girl in a swimsuit with a ribbon across her chest was smiling at us.

"Hooray for the team!" the bearded man shouted. "Come on, get up here!"

Manny climbed the steps, and I followed him. "Come on, team—the rest of you get up here!" He smiled at Millicent. "You too. You're part of the team, aren't you?"

Everyone lined up behind Manny and me, while the bearded man shook hands with us. "May I present myself? My name is Orson Bean. And I want to introduce you to Valerie Clark, Miss Downhill Invitational."

The girl came to stand at the microphone with us. Orson Bean held up a shiny trophy. "Brad, I want to present this magnificent trophy to you in honor of your winning the First Annual Downhill Invitational Championship."

I hesitated, looking at Manny. The trophy was for the whole team, after all.

"Take it, Brad," Manny told me. "You've earned it."

I accepted the trophy and spoke into the mike. "Thank you for all of the Los Angeles Wheels." Then I passed it around so everyone could see it.

Orson Bean reached into his pocket and pulled out a white envelope. "And to Emanuel Bloom and members of the team, I have a check here, the winning prize money—twenty thousand dollars. Congratulations!"

Manny took the envelope and kissed it. "Twenty grand! Thank you!"

I'd never seen him look happier.

Miss Downhill Invitational gave us a kiss; the band started playing something louder and more cheerful, and the crowd roared wildly. As we went down the steps, a group of teen-agers surrounded us, reaching out to touch us and to get a look at the trophy. I was so busy, I didn't notice until later that Manny was nowhere in sight.

Chapter 27

Sol hadn't wasted any time. The minute Manny stepped off the platform and the crowd surrounded the team, he felt someone pulling his arm. It was Sol's friend.

He escorted Manny to a secluded spot, away from the crowd, where Sol was waiting. Manny, for once, was happy to see him.

"You thought you wouldn't get your money, didn't you?"

"All right . . . all right." Sol held out his hand, palm up.

"You owe me an apology," Manny said cheerfully.

"All right."

Manny poked a finger at Sol's chest. "Was I on the level or not?"

"Okay, big shot . . . the money." Sol pushed Manny's finger aside.

Manny pulled the envelope out of his pocket and started to open it, but the henchman grabbed it out of his hand and passed it to Sol's waiting fingers.

Sol opened it and pulled out a piece of green paper. "This is a check!"

"What did you expect? Used tens?" Manny chuckled.

"You know I don't take checks."

"Don't worry, it's good. It's not mine."

The henchman made a menacing move toward Manny, but Sol reached a hand out to stop him. "It's okay. It's a cashier's check." He pulled a wallet out of his back pocket. "I owe you ten."

"That's funny," Manny said. "That's hysterical. *You* owe *me* ten thousand dollars. It should happen every day, Sol!"

Sol counted out the money in Manny's hand, and shook his head. "You know, I have to say something. I've never seen anybody take a roll on the dice like you just did!"

Manny grinned and started to walk away, but Sol's big hand fell on his shoulder to stop him. "Just do me one favor."

"Anything, Sol. I'd do anything for you. You know that." That was true. Manny felt so good at this minute he'd do anything for anybody.

"Stay away from me," Sol said, moving toward the parking lot.

"See you, Bloom" the henchman said, following.

"Not if I see you first!" Manny watched them walking across the grass, then he turned and headed for the bus. This would be the biggest, happiest celebration he'd ever had.

He made his way through the thinning crowd. The team was waiting for him, standing beside the bus, handing out autographs to the fans who still surrounded them.

"Hey! Give them a break!" Manny said to the

fans. "Hop in, Brad. You too, Tony. Come on, everybody!"

They got inside the bus and Manny reached for the styrofoam cooler under the front seat.

Brad slapped him on the back. "We're champs! Real champs!"

Grinning, Manny brought out several bottles of champagne and handed them to Millicent. She popped the cork of the first one and poured the contents into paper cups, handing them to the team members.

"What a day!" Tony said, swallowing his in one gulp.

"What a race!" Jenny agreed.

"And here's one of the best parts." Manny pulled the money out of his pocket. He counted out seven piles of bills and put the rest of the money, a much smaller wad, back in his pocket.

"Yippee!" Brad drank his champagne and took his share of the money. "Primo!"

"Millicent, here's your back pay." Manny handed her one of the stacks. "Jenny, Tony, everybody. These are even shares."

"Yeowee!" Tony yelped. "We're the greatest!" He socked Brad's arm. "Right, champ?"

They all thought so, and said so all at once. They drank the champagne and talked about the team going to New York and Las Vegas. Dennis and Peter doused Manny with the contents of one of the bottles, until he grabbed it from them and drank what was left, complaining that he didn't know how anyone could like this stuff.

Suddenly the laughter and talking died away. Manny looked up, wondering what was going on, and saw everyone staring at the door of the bus.

Jason stood just outside.

Manny pulled the control that opened the door, but Jason stayed where he was. "Hi, Manny. How're you doing?"

"Fine. How are *you* doing, kid?"

"Oh, fine." Jason was obviously embarrassed. "I just came by to congratulate everybody."

"Well come on in," Manny said. "We've been worried about you."

Jason stepped slowly inside the bus. He was greeted with silence. Nobody seemed to know what to say.

Then Randi ran to him, put her arms around him, and kissed him. Manny saw Brad's face as she did this. Poor kid looked hurt, but just for a moment. Then Brad smiled and came forward toward Jason.

"You should have been here sooner. You missed the best performance the Los Angeles Wheels have put on yet."

Jason looked uncomfortable. "I saw it all," he said. "You bet it was the best! And you were really ripping, Brad!" Then he raised his voice so everyone on the bus could hear him. "I came by to apologize to all of you. I've had a few problems, but I think I've got my head on straight now. And I'd like to ask if you'll still have me on the team. I promise not to drop out again like I just did."

That must have been hard for him, Manny thought. For the first time he realized he'd been so wrapped up in his own troubles, he hadn't thought about what Jason might be going through. He wanted to hug the kid and tell him that he sure could come back with the team, but he wanted to know how the others felt first. He said nothing, and waited.

Jenny was the first to speak. "Welcome back, Jason!"

"Sit down, man!" Tony said. "Zip the lip and sit down!"

Then everyone was talking, so Manny held up his hand for quiet. "Sounds like we're all glad to have you back," he said.

For the first time, Jason smiled. "Thanks. I think I proved one thing, anyway. The L.A. Wheels is a great team . . . with me or without me.'

"What do you say we vote Jason a full share of the money?" Brad said.

There was a chorus of voices answering: "Sure!" "Great!" and then, as the talking and laughing resumed and Jason was given some champagne, Brad turned to Manny.

"Would you have been mad at me if I'd lost?"

Manny grinned at him. "Come on, Brad. You know me better than that! I would have died laughing!" He leaned back against the dashboard of the bus and folded his arms. "Now would everybody shut up, I'll tell you what I've got planned for us next." Tony slipped off his earphones at that moment and asked, "Yea Manny, what's our next gig?"

Manny, still excited and slightly confused, put his hands to his champagne drenched head, looked around at the happy faces in the bus and admitted joyfully, "I don't know!" But he knew . . . the L.A. Wheels were hot and had a big future.

* * *

I suppose you would say that the story of the L.A. Wheels has a happy ending; but for me it was much more than that. There were a lot of things I learned about myself. I guess you could say I grew up.

At first, even though the other kids on the team were my friends, I thought they were somehow all better than me. Not just better skateboarders, but smarter, more courageous and streetwise, and most of all more together. That summer I found out that each one of them had some of the same problems I did. They too, were still sorting things out, learning how to face their weaknesses and cope. Suddenly, I saw my friends as real people, not superheros. I learned that I was just as valuable to them as they were to me. We all needed to rely on and trust one another. We especially had to understand and help each other through tough times. Like the time Jason, who I thought was just the coolest guy going down, really needed our support. I'd never take anybody at face value again.

Another thing I found out was that being unsure of myself was definitely not a good excuse for laying back and not trying my best. Like a flash, I understood that I was the kind of person who always tried my best, until the time I took the blame for losing that Little League game long ago. Ever since that game I was afraid to go all out for fear I wouldn't live up to my parents' expectations. Now I no longer felt guilty for losing that game. I realized I had done my best and if we lost, it was because the other team was better or maybe luckier, but not because I failed. I knew now that I had played to win, not just to please my parents. That's the important thing.

So the story of my skateboard summer had more than one happy ending for me. I'm proud to be a member of the L.A. Wheels great skateboard team, but even more than that I'm proud to be myself, Brad Harris.

TIPS FROM PROFESSIONAL
SKATEBOARDERS

ELLEN ONEAL, who played the part of "Jenny Bradshaw" in the film *Skateboard*, started riding a skateboard when she was fourteen. She had a summer job with the *San Diego Union Tribune*, and would use her skateboard as she made collections for the paper route. Then the paper sponsored a skateboarding contest, and Ellen's friends and family encouraged her to enter. She found herself the only female contestant registered with seventy males, but she summoned up her courage and won second place. Since then she has gone on to win freestyle championships, including the 1977 California Freeformer World Championship at Long Beach, California. As well as being a member of Gordon and Smith's demonstration team, she writes a regular column for *Skateworld Journal*.

Ellen began skateboarding in a cul-de-sac in her quiet neighborhood, in a church parking lot that was empty most days except Sunday, and in a large parking lot by the beach that was empty during off-business hours. She does not advise using roads or streets for skateboarding. Pick traffic-free spots. Even school grounds can be used during times the school is empty.

Ellen feels her five years of studying ballet and her experience on the school gymnastics team helped a great deal to teach her good balance and to give her freestyle routine a "fluid" look. She advises beginners to start slowly, practice hard, and not try anything they're not positive they can do. As she put it: "Be sure you can swim before you go to the deep end of the swimming pool."

While Ellen feels skateboarding is becoming a much safer sport through the use of skateboard parks and safety equipment, she says the dangerous aspect is what makes it exciting. It takes skill and ability, and this gives the skateboarder pride in developing good physical coordination.

As for equipment—Ellen did not wear safety gear as a beginner. She feels you're not too likely to get hurt if you remember to take the easy things first. She likes a stiff board with a stiff flex, not too wide a truck base, and medium wheels for freestyle maneuvers. When you're advanced enough to do bank riding, a light wooden board of multiplex laminate, wide, and with a heavier truck, is best.

She advises beginners to use concentration—put your whole self into what you're doing. She feels she can tell the difference in her performance on days when she doesn't use all her concentration, and she usually practices an hour a day, every day she can, with three to four hours a day practice before competitions. But Ellen adds that you should never forget the main reason for skateboarding: *It's fun.* Don't make it such hard work that it isn't fun anymore, even in a competition.

At the Skateboard Safety Clinic held in Century City, California, in November 1977, several skateboarders kindly consented to pass along these tips:

RUSS HOWELL, 28, of Long Beach, California, has won many championships, among them the 1975 U.S. National Freestyle Championship. He holds the 1977 World Consecutive Three-Sixties record, and heads the Russ Howell Skateboard Team. Russ has traveled extensively, talking about and demonstrating the sport of skateboarding. He was conducting the safety clinic, and says that freestyle skateboarding is the safest form of this sport as well as the most lucrative, from a professional point of view. The skill involved in freestyle takes longer to learn, but pays most for personal appearances. He doesn't care for downhill racing because of the speeds and consequent dangers involved. He says that while he enjoys the skill and physical dexterity expended in skateboarding, he doesn't want to get hurt, and for that reason, too, he chooses freestyle. He compares this with such sports as football, in which "a bunch of guys are likely to pile on top of you and hurt you," and to baseball, in which you have to please a coach and work with your teammates.

Most skateboarders seem to enjoy being loners, but Russ feels that wherever you're skating you should be aware of where you are in time and space, and observe who and what is around you. He advises skaters not to think you're the only one on the street or in the park, and just because you've got your feet on a skateboard, don't think everyone else is watching you. Being aware will prevent accidents.

Russ has been skateboarding since he was ten years old. He feels this generation of "free spirits" likes skateboarding because it allows them to be creative, to do their own thing, and physically to express themselves.

Russ says skateboarding has been a good friend to him, showing him what's inside of him and how to express it. On the practical side, he told us that when he travels, he might be the last person off the plane, but is always first to the terminal. He rides his skateboard!

STACY PERALTA, 20, of Santa Monica, who is a champion skateboarder says beginners should start slowly and work their way up. Don't go overboard trying to do the difficult things first; they'll come more easily as your skills develop. He advises skaters to relax. If you're too tense, it's more difficult to do the movements.

Stacy feels skateboarding is a form of self-expression. You put everything into it that you've got, and you can go into your own trip. You're totally free—no one is interfering with you. He does feel, however, that it's inspiring to be with a team.

PAUL HOFFMAN, 16, of Redondo Beach, has won first place in the Northern California Freestyle Competition in both 1976 and 1977; first place in the Orange County Fairgrounds Slalom; first place in the Santa Monica Championship Freestyle; second place in the World Three-Sixties

Championship Competition at Long Beach, California.

Paul says skateboarding keeps his body in top condition and improves his surfing. He advises skaters to use safety equipment all the time; stay out of empty pools because of the dangers involved, even for advanced skaters; and make sure that the ground, wherever you skate, is free of pebbles and debris that could cause you to fall.

STEVE DAY, 17, of Downey, is a member of the Russ Howell Skateboard Team. He started skateboarding three years ago in a park near his house, and once broke his arm skating without equipment. Now he wears knee and elbow pads, wrist braces, and gloves, and advises skaters always to wear shoes.

Steve says to take it easy at first, and use the best equipment you can afford. For bank riding, use a wooden kicktail board with large wheels. For freestyle, Steve feels a fiberglass board is best, with smaller wheels. To find out which skateboard is best for you, read the skateboard magazines, go to demonstrations, talk to pros and other skaters and see what they recommend. He says a good board can cost from $40 up.

He thinks beginners should start with freestyle skating rather than bank riding, to develop their form and expertise first. Bank riding can be dangerous, he points out, and requires no special skill except daring. When bank riding, Steve feels that you shouldn't do "flyouts" or "popouts" (riding up the bank and over it), or "fakies" (riding the bank without kick turning at the top, just going straight down again). These tricks are dangerous.

He would advise everyone to join a team, but this has to come after your skills have been developed enough. He says if you go to the places where the pros meet, such as skateboard parks, they'll notice you if you're good enough and invite you to join their teams.

We visited Skateboard World Park in Torrance, California, which has large areas of concrete flat surfaces, bowls, runs, half pipes, and even a slope that was equipped with movable plastic cones for slalom practicing. Bins of elbow and knee pads, gloves, and helmets waited at the gate for the use of skateboarders, and their use is required. While there, we met and talked with several of the skateboarders.

GENE RIEHLE, winner of the California State Championship in 1975, is now on the Ampul team. Gene showed us some expert bank riding, and his special trick which, he tells us, is not done by anyone else: two kick turns at the top of the bank, instead of the usual one.

Gene compares skateboarding with surfing, but says it's better than rollerskating, since he "likes four wheels instead of eight." He advises beginners to take it slow at first, to build up proficiency and endurance.

Gene uses an aluminum skateboard because he likes its lightness and maneuverability, but he pointed out that the edges of the board had been worn into jagged points, and mentioned he knew this was unsafe.

JAY SIMPSON, 20, of Costa Mesa, says you must know your own limits. Get your kick turns perfected on flat surfaces before you try bank riding, for instance. He feels that skateboard parks are the best places to practice, for several reasons. First of all, safety equipment is required at all times, usually furnished by the park. Then Jay pointed out that if anyone is injured in a skateboard park, first aid will be given on the spot. If you are riding alone somewhere else you might get an injury, and perhaps you won't be able to get help right away. He also noted that these parks are exclusively for skateboarders, so there are no pedestrians or vehicles to watch out for.

Jay says that skateboarding can sometimes be dangerous, so use safety precautions. For him, one of the biggest attractions in skateboarding is the weightless sensation he gets from it.

ARTHUR SANDOVAL, 15, started skating on the patio in his backyard. He now has a half pipe that he made himself of plywood, and practices there about an hour and a half per day.

Arthur describes skateboarding as a "total rush." He advises beginners to get the best wooden board they can afford, and stay away from the plastic "cheapies."

CHERYL BEAUCHAMP, 39, of Pasadena, feels that skateboarding is not exclusively for males or for teen-agers, but can be a feminine sport and good for you at any age. She started skateboarding for exercise.

The first time she tried to get on a skateboard,

she set it on her lawn so that the board would move but not too quickly. Then she practiced standing on it, and balancing, before she tried rolling it.

Cheryl feels that one of the biggest attractions of skateboarding is that it can be done right around home. You don't have to travel to the beach or the ski runs. She says it's been a fantastic experience for her to find out what her body was capable of doing, and recommends skateboarding to everyone.

TONY "MAD DOG" ALVA, 20, the men's overall world professional skateboarding champion, has a large following among skateboarders in this country. Featured as Tony Bluetile in Universal's "Skateboard," he helped bring the grace, daring and excitement of this fast-growing sport to a wider audience.

The outspoken self-styled "radical Dogtowner" (tough kid from Santa Monica) is credited with developing the new, aggressive style of skateboarding.

"It's a total surfing style," he says. "Surfing and skating to me are skin tight, both together. There aren't too many big waves around here, so you have to be aggressive out in the water. I just regenerate that same energy and aggressiveness into skateboarding."

Alva, who has leaped over 18 barrels on his board (a world record), defied gravity on the 25-foot high sides of drainage pipes and performed such stunts as U-turns standing on his head, won his title in overall competition in downhill and slalom racing, vertical and flatland freestyle and performing in a concrete bowl.

For his own fun, he prefers "tail-tapping"—riding a skateboard into the deep end of an empty swimming pool, skating up the opposite side until all four wheels are over the edge, then tapping the back edge of the board, skating back down and up the other side.

"That's where the heavy sensations are," he says. "When you skate pools just right and just full-on attack them, really hitting the lines—frontside, backside, off-the-lip, cutback, etc.—it's like flying. The weightless phases are really intense."

Even with such safety equipment as helmets, elbow and knee pads, and long gloves, injuries are not uncommon, but professional skaters seldom fall. "A good pool rider knows when to bail," he says. "I push it as far as it's safe for me."